Motioning for Tomas Mendoza to stay where he was, Joe Howard eased to the edge of the outcropping. From there he could see five men spreading out on the canyon floor below. He could have picked them off one by one but that wasn't the way he wanted to do things.

He could see that Winston Haverty was backing away from the group as if he wanted the others to take all the risks. It would be easier to take him than Joe had first thought. He eased down the north side of the outcropping and moments later was standing directly behind Haverty. He stood still until Haverty had almost backed into his arms, then pressed the rifle barrel against Haverty's back.

"I'd like nothing better than to kill you right here," Joe said in a low voice. "Tell your boys to drop their guns."

Before Haverty could call out, a gun barked and Joe heard an oath yelled in Spanish. Looking up at the outcropping, he saw Tomas Mendoza grab at his chest and fall to the ground.

It was all Joe could do to keep from pulling the trigger. "Call your men," he repeated in a low growl. "Call them or so help me I'll kill you right here!"

FOR THE BEST OF THE WEST—
DAN PARKINSON

A MAN CALLED WOLF   (2794, $3.95)
Somewhere in the scorched southwestern frontier where civilization was just a step away from the dark ages, an army of hired guns was restoring the blood cult of an ancient empire. Only one man could stop them: John Thomas Wolf.

THE WAY TO WYOMING   (2411, $3.95)
Matt Hazlewood and Big Jim Tyson had fought side by side wearing the gray ten years before. Now, with a bloody range war closing in fast behind and killers up ahead, they'd join up to ride and fight again in an untamed land where there was just the plains, the dust, and the heat— and the law of the gun!

GUNPOWDER WIND   (2456, $3.95)
by Dan Parkinson and David Hicks
War was brewing between the Anglo homesteaders and the town's loco Mexican commander Colonel Piedras. Figuring to keep the settlers occupied with a little Indian trouble, Piedras had Cherokee warrior Utsada gunned down in cold blood. Now it was up to young Cooper Willoughby to find him before the Cherokees hit the warpath!

THE WESTERING   (2559, $3.95)
There were laws against settin' a blood bounty on an innocent man, but Frank Kingston did it anyway, and Zack Frost found himself hightailin' it out of Indiana with a price on his head and a pack of bloodthirsty bounty hunters hot on his trail!

BIG BEND AMBUSH

ERLE ADKINS

ZEBRA BOOKS
KENSINGTON PUBLISHING CORP.

ZEBRA BOOKS

are published by

Kensington Publishing Corp.
475 Park Avenue South
New York, NY 10016

First printing: June, 1991

Printed in the United States of America

Chapter 1

Long stealthy shadows crept across the dusty parade ground at Fort Davis, Texas, and clawed their way up the jagged granite mountains. A warm afternoon breeze swept over the vast mountainous desert and stirred up the powderlike dust, throwing particles at the two men sitting on the front porch of the fort headquarters.

"Did you ever get the feeling that you were only put on this earth to settle the problems of other people?" Colonel Eric McRaney asked pensively. He leaned back in the straight wooden chair, crossed his long legs at the ankles on the porch railing, and laced his long fingers behind his head as he looked up at the blue sky. A few white clouds that were touched with gold and pink eased along on the air currents.

Something told Joe Howard that when McRaney began talking philosophically, he was about to be sent somewhere to become involved in someone else's problem. It always worked out like that and this time would probably be no different.

Joe had known McRaney for a long time and knew that he enjoyed using subtle suggestions or taking the long way around to finally tell him what to do. The situation usually ended up with Joe feeling like he'd either instigated his involvement in a situation or volunteered for it.

In either event, Joe knew that the longer McRaney talked, the longer he'd be able to sit on the porch and do nothing.

"Yeah," Joe finally answered, slouching down in the chair and crossing his right leg over his left knee. He glanced over at McRaney and mentally shook his head. The tall colonel always managed to look as if he'd just bathed and changed clothes. The only thing that attested to the fact that McRaney had worn the same dark blue uniform with a yellow stripe down the legs since early morning was the film of dust on the black calf-length boots. His thick black hair was neatly combed back from his narrow forehead and the jaw-length black sideburns were trimmed close to his face. But after all, Joe placated himself, the main reason for McRaney's clean looks was that the only thing he'd been pushing all morning was a pen over paper.

Joe Howard, on the other hand, looked like a dusty bum. He had been pushing his horse, Serge, on a dusty ride from El Paso. His light brown hair needed to be cut. It was hanging down past his collar and his thin, angular, tanned face was covered with a two-day growth of light brown beard. His light blue shirt was sweat-stained and his dark blue pants were dust-stained. His black, flat-crowned hat didn't look too bad, though, considering it was at least five years old.

"Did you ever wonder why there are so many problems in this world?" Joe asked, taking in a lung full of the crisp mountain air. "Just look out there." He made a wide sweeping gesture with his right hand that encompassed the vast openness. "There's enough space between here and El Paso for all of us. If you and I and every soldier here at the fort had a section of land, we could live in the middle of it and never have to see anybody unless we really wanted to."

McRaney turned his head slowly and looked at Joe with a slight frown pulling lines between his thin black brows. He closed his eyes slowly and opened them. "You've got a point there," McRaney agreed, nodding slowly and making a smacking sound with his mouth. "But," he continued, drawing the word out and narrowing his slate-blue eyes, "what if I found a gold vein on my section of land? What if that particular section of land joined yours?" McRaney arched his brows as he watched Joe run this thumb thoughtfully along his chin. Every positive solution always had a negative side.

"You just drive me crazy when you make sense," Joe said, drawing his mouth into a smirking line and frowning sarcastically at McRaney. "Do you know that?" Joe sat up straight in the chair, slammed his feet down against the floor, and shook his head slowly.

McRaney threw back his head and his booming laughter echoed out across the parade ground.

"Well, what would you do?" McRaney insisted,

7

coughing and clearing his throat. He lowered his feet from the railing and stretched his legs out before him. "Wouldn't your human greed take over your pride of land ownership and space?"

"That's probably a foregone conclusion," Joe answered, grinning at McRaney. "How big would this vein of gold be?"

This time both men laughed until their eyes were misty. When they finally regained their composure, Joe glanced over at McRaney and could tell from the sly expression on his face that the colonel was about to drop the other boot, as it were, on him. Maybe if he didn't say anything, McRaney wouldn't be so quick to find something else for him to do. Joe was of the opinion that it galled McRaney to see him idle for very long. But Joe knew that his time had run out when McRaney took a long breath, sat up straight in the chair, and looked at Joe sideways.

"Do you remember Chief Keoni, the Indian you met when you first came to Fort Davis?" McRaney asked, narrowing his eyes and rolling his mouth in against his teeth. He could almost read the scout's mind, and a sly grin pulled at his lips.

Here it comes, Joe thought grimly as he nodded. He wondered if he was going to be sent to meet this Indian all of the way, or part of the way, or to get him out of some kind of trouble.

"Yeah, I remember him," Joe said, pushing his hat back on his head. "Why? What does he have to do with gold?" He knew the Indian had nothing to do with gold, but he would use any means to stall for time.

"He doesn't have anything to do with gold," McRaney said glibly, standing up, walking to the edge of the porch, and leaning against the white wooden support. He shoved his hands down into his pockets and hunched his shoulders a little before saying anything else. Finally he turned back around and looked at Joe. "Do you also remember Senator Caleb Powers, the one who Keoni was going to meet at Langtry to discuss a way to stop the raids on wagon trains and stages between El Paso and San Antonio?"

Joe had remembered taking a letter to the Apache chief which summoned him to meet with Powers. Keoni had suggested to Joe that Powers meet with him and McRaney at the fort.

But so much had happened to Joe Howard since that proposed meeting was to have taken place that he'd completely forgotten about it until now. "Yeah, I remember, now that you've mentioned it. You called Powers a pompous ass," Joe said, hoping against hope that what he was thinking was wrong. It was one thing to get involved with Indians. It was one thing to get involved with state senators and such. But when the two things meshed together, that was a whole other story.

"What has one thing got to do with the other?" Joe asked, feeling a knot pulling in his stomach. He knew that his time of idleness was about to end. "Did Keoni and Powers ever have their meeting?" He remembered Keoni telling him that it would be no more an imposition for Powers to come to Fort Davis than it would be for him to go to Langtry.

"Oh, yeah," McRaney drawled out contemptuously, and nodded slowly. "Keoni had no choice and finally gave in and met with that fat head at Langtry. I hope you meet Powers someday." McRaney's slate-blue eyes turned darker and snapped in anger. He expelled a ragged breath.

"And?" Joe prompted, a little baffled at McRaney's attitude.

"Chief Keoni," McRaney said resolutely, turning around and facing Joe, "told Powers that he would do all he could to stop the raids if the government would help them with food. Especially meat. It is Keoni's belief that, with so much travel through here, what little game that was available has been scared off. The buffalo in particular."

The buffalo was such a vital part of the Indian lifestyle that probably the only portion of it that wasn't used was the grunt and smell. The government would help him with food and the Indian would help the government by staying in one place for food.

But that was where Joe's thinking differed from the government's. He had begun to realize that anything that appeared simple to the common man had to be turned into a round-table discussion if the government was involved in it.

"So," Joe urged, leaning back in the chair and crossing his legs again. The longer it took McRaney to tell him about the situation, the longer he could set there. He knew that someone would end up getting killed. It could be him.

"So meat began arriving to the Indians," McRaney continued, looking down at Joe and arching his black brows. "Keoni said at first the meat was good.

Then the quantity and quality began deteriorating."

Something began happening way in the back of Joe's mind but he couldn't quite put words to it. "What do you mean?" he asked, looking up at McRaney and frowning. A strange feeling raced up Joe's back and he could almost feel the hairs standing up on the back of his neck.

"Keoni told me last week that the last shipment of meat was just a shade from being rotten." McRaney's thin-lipped mouth curled up with disgust.

"Rotten?" Joe asked, feeling his own skin crawl. "How could the meat be rotten? How is the meat gotten to the Indians?" Joe asked, feeling his stomach turn over. "Where does the meat come from? How far does it have to go?"

Somehow Joe had gotten the impression that Keoni's camp was only a few miles from the fort and the town of the same name, Fort Davis. Getting the cattle to the fort and then to the Indians would be no problem. But there again, simplicity set in and he knew that it wasn't very likely to happen like that.

"Joe," McRaney said with good-humored sarcasm, exasperation in his eyes, "you can ask more questions than a schoolteacher. Your father must have been a lawyer." McRaney pressed his mouth into a thin line and glared down at Joe, a good-natured glare in his eyes. "The meat, which is salted, arrives by wagons. Keoni has moved his people over to Elephant Mountain on Calamity Creek. That's about a three-day ride south of here," McRaney explained to the frown on Joe's face.

Joe knew that McRaney was getting closer to his

part in this situation and his heart began slamming against his ribs.

"By wagon?" Joe repeated. Joe stared up at McRaney for a couple of seconds and batted his eyes. "Now that's the stupidest thing I've ever heard of," Joe said, shaking his head slowly and in derision. He would have been a lot better off if he had just hushed right then and let McRaney finish telling him about the Indians, the meat, and the government in his own way.

But that wasn't and would never be Joe Howard's way of doing things. It was his nature to try and jump into the middle of the river without testing to see how deep it was by slowly wading out.

"Why aren't the cattle just driven to Elephant Mountain?" Joe asked, standing up and walking to the edge of the porch, then turning around and facing McRaney. "That way the meat would certainly be fresh when it got there. Keoni could discard what he didn't want, which would probably be very little."

"Joe," McRaney said in a placating tone of voice and gesturing with his palms up, "you should know by now, and as well as I do, that the government doesn't work like that." Then he gave words to Joe's thoughts. "That would be too simple. That would be only enough paperwork for a couple of men."

Joe looked at McRaney and grinned. Joe knew that he could probably get the whole thing done in just a little while with about six civilian riders, whereas it would take the army a month with an entire platoon. No doubt McRaney knew what Joe was thinking because there was a steady gleam in his eyes. Something told Joe that he was about to get that opportunity.

"Where am I supposed to start checking on the meat?" Joe asked, removing his hat, pushing his hair back, and replacing the hat. "Who do I see first and when do I meet with Keoni?"

An awe-stricken look gaped McRaney's mouth as he looked at Joe. "Your brain must be entirely worn out by the time you go to bed at night," McRaney said, shaking his head slowly and narrowing his eyes until wrinkles appeared at the corners. Unexpectedly, he reached out and patted Joe on the forehead.

"Well, you don't learn unless you ask," Joe said grimly, feeling his face turn red.

"The cattle are driven to Marathon," McRaney continued, a tight smile pulling at his mouth. "Before you ask, I don't know from where. They're supposed to be butchered there, dressed out, salted down, put into wagons, and then driven to Elephant Mountain." McRaney held up his hand when he saw Joe take a breath to ask another question. "An agreement"—he ducked his head to one side and arched his brows—"between Senator Powers and Chief Keoni gives the Indians three thousand pounds of meat every three months. In exchange for the meat, Keoni's braves would stop the raiding because that would take care of the buffalo that was lost."

Joe's spinning mind digested McRaney's explanation. With that much meat in an Indian camp, along with the small game they usually got, the Indians shouldn't have much to worry about. But McRaney

13

had said two words which would destroy the entire concept: "an agreement." Ever since that white man had given that Indian some beads and a few coins for Manhattan Island, no agreement had been worth the paper it was written on or the effort required to write it.

"If the meat is salted properly," Joe said, pursing his mouth thoughtfully, looking up at the clear blue sky, "and nothing happens between Marathon and Elephant Mountain, the meat should be good when it gets there. I still don't understand," he said, shaking his head slowly, "why the cattle aren't just driven to the Indians. That would be less trouble and mess for whoever is doing it. The cattle might lose a few pounds, but the Indians would get more out of the cows than just meat."

"That's what I want you to find out," McRaney said, watching Joe intently.

A thought suddenly struck Joe and he jerked his attention back to the colonel. "How soon do you want me to start for Marathon?" For some reason, he was glad and his heart began racing when McRaney said, "Right away."

Taking long strides, Joe kicked through the dust across the parade ground to the barracks. It didn't take long for him to pull his saddle bags from under the wooden bunk and stuff in some clothes and ammunition. He had plenty of shells for the Colt .45 strapped around his lean waist and tied to his muscular thigh but would have to stop at the general store in Fort Davis for shells for the Winchester. Joe's last stop before going to the corral was the mess hall.

14

The big, burly, redheaded cook put a skillet, coffee pot, flour, salt meat, and a sack of coffee into the grub sack, along with a can of peaches.

"Where are you off to this time?" Gibbons asked in a gruff voice, a little envy in his bloodshot green eyes. His red-veined, bulbous nose gave credence to the fact that he had a penchant for whiskey, whether the good or the cheapest rotgut. He couldn't be as old as his wrinkled face said he was.

"Oh, I've got to see an Indian about a cow," Joe replied, pouring steaming black coffee from the well-used coffeepot into a blue and white speckled cup.

"You must be talking about the bad meat that chief Keoni and his people have been getting from the government," Gibbons said, disgust in his observation as he pulled the drawstring tight on the grub sack and put it on the table.

"Yeah," Joe answered, nodding, more than a little surprised at the sympathy in the big man's voice. Gibbons was probably in the minority as far as feelings went for Indians. Good feelings, that is. "Something just doesn't make sense to me about the whole thing," Joe continued. "If the meat is handled properly, it shouldn't rot so fast."

"Well, good luck," Gibbons said as Joe picked up the grub sack and started toward the door. "I imagine that you're going to need it."

"Thanks," Joe called out over his shoulder. Reaching the corral, he put a blanket and saddle on the almost seal-black horse, tied the saddlebags and bedroll on, and filled a water canteen from a trough outside the corral.

"Well, Serge," Joe said, swinging up and patting the long sleek neck, "it looks like we've got a long way to go to see why some Indians are being cheated out of some food." A shiver raced up and down Joe's back. In his mind's eye he could see green tainted meat with brown things crawling all over it.

The black horse rumbled low in his throat and tossed his head. He seemed to understand everything that Joe Howard said to him.

The town of Fort Davis was only a short distance from the fort and it didn't take Joe long to reach Upshaw's General Store. Joe dismounted, tied Serge to the wooden hitch rail, stepped up on the plank sidewalk, and entered the cluttered building.

"I need some shells for my Winchester," Joe said when Titus Upshaw came from the back. The tall, thin, balding man put two galvanized buckets down on the counter and reached behind him to a shelf for the shells.

"I guess you're going out on another job, huh?" Upshaw stated more than asked when he handed Joe the box.

"Yeah," Joe answered, smiling at the storekeeper. "Colonel McRaney can't stand to see me sitting still very long. He wants to be sure that I earn my pay."

Once again Joe Howard would have been better off if he'd hushed right then and left well enough alone. But he didn't. "I've got to see about some Indians and cattle."

Upshaw's bony fingers tightened on the shell box until his knuckles turned white. "If I had my way about it, those blasted Indians could starve to death. I

16

just don't understand why the government has to feed all of the redskinned savages.''

Upshaw's brown eyes were blazing, his thin face was almost purple in rage, and a knot worked in his jaw. His voice was cold. There was a white circle around his tightly compressed mouth.

"The government is feeding them because of an agreement," Joe answered slowly in a firm and grating tone. He slapped some money down on the counter and started to pick up the box of shells.

"Hang the agreement!" Upshaw shouted, his eyes blazing. "Hang the Indians. Every last one of them! And I don't have anything good to say about anyone who helps them."

Before Joe Howard knew what was happening, Titus Upshaw charged around the end of the counter, grabbed him by the front of his blue shirt, and gave him a punch in the face that brought hot salty blood into his mouth. Joe hadn't known Titus Upshaw very long but nothing in their short acquaintance would have prepared him for this surprise attack. Joe stepped backward, pulling out of Upshaw's grasp, and stared at the half-crazy man. He was breathing hard through his thin nose and there was a dazed expression in his eyes.

"I don't care whether you have anything good to say about me or not," Joe growled, a glare in his brown eyes that would almost pull the stink from a skunk. "But an agreement is an agreement. What in the devil is wrong with you anyway?" Joe asked, wiping his hand across his cut mouth.

"I don't like Indians," Upshaw answered in a tense

17

voice. "I never have. All they want to do is kill people and burn houses."

"Don't you sort of think you're in the wrong place then?" Joe asked castigatingly, reaching out for the shells on the counter.

"I've got a right to be wherever I want to be," Upshaw snapped back, glaring at Joe. Joe held the almost deranged man's gaze until red embarrassment crept up his thin face. Upshaw dropped his gaze when he realized what he'd just said.

Joe, knowing that he'd made a point without saying anything else, walked slowly over to the door. He just couldn't let Upshaw's attack go by without some retaliation but knew that tearing into the bigoted man wouldn't make any difference.

"Upshaw," Joe began in a steady voice, "I don't know, nor do I care, why your attitude is like this, but the next time you lay a hand on me for any reason, I swear to God that I'll kill you."

Without waiting for Upshaw's reaction, Joe stomped out of the store, swung up on Serge, and started east toward Marathon.

"That man has to be crazy," Joe said aloud, spitting out blood. Joe could feel his mouth swelling and knew that it would be sore for a long time. "Not that I wanted to waste time in asking him, but I wonder what caused him to feel so much hatred toward Indians. Wonder why he wanted to settle in the big middle of them in the first place?"

Serge tossed his head at the sound of Joe's voice and the army scout grinned.

Joe knew that he couldn't reach Marathon before late evening tomorrow but decided to ride a few hours after the sun had gone down. It would be a little cooler on both him and Serge and they could make some good time. The sooner this was settled, the better he would like it.

Darkness had settled over the land about two hours earlier when he finally pulled Serge to a stop under a juniper tree to spend the night. Joe unsaddled Serge, opened up the grub sack, and took out just the coffeepot, coffee, and cup. He wasn't all that hungry and didn't want to go to all the trouble of making bread and cooking meat tonight.

A sobering thought struck him as he sipped the coffee. Here he had plenty of good meat to cook but wasn't going to because of the trouble involved. He wondered if the Indians even had any meat to cook.

He poured only enough water into the pot for one cup of coffee and built only a very small fire. It didn't occur to him that he might be in any danger as he leaned back against the saddle with his legs crossed, enjoying the coffee and listening to the night sounds.

Joe had spent so much time out in the open with the mingled sounds around him that at first they all seemed to be one. But as he listened closer, he heard each distinct sound. An owl asked its question. A dove cooed. A cougar screamed. And finally, to Joe anyway, came the most beautiful yet loneliest sound of them all—the coyote's cry. All of that was mixed in with the crickets' singing and the whisper of the never-ceasing wind.

But suddenly Joe's heart almost stopped and his blood ran cold as his ears picked up a more distinctive sound that had nothing to do with animal or insect. Joe hadn't given any particular care to where he had stopped because he hadn't thought he would need to. But he wished now that he'd chosen a place with a little more protection.

As it was, he was right out in the open, sitting under a tree and having a cup of coffee just as comfortably as if he'd been sitting in a restaurant in Denver. He strained his ears and listened again, hoping that he was wrong about what he'd heard. Every pore in his body was oozing sweat. He heard the sound again. Someone was definitely out there. But why was he walking?

Knowing that he was like a sitting duck in the glow of the small fire, Joe jumped up, yanked the rifle from the scabbard on the saddle, and backed up against the tree.

"Whoever you are," he called out with a lot more courage in his voice than he felt as he slammed a shell into the chamber of the rifle, "I'm an army scout out of Fort Davis." He knew that would make a lot of difference. "Step into the firelight so that I can see you."

Joe could hear his heart beating in his ears but he could also hear the steps again. They had a more purposeful sound now. "I'm going to count to three before I start shooting." Joe, who was only twenty-three, wondered if it was true that the good usually die young.

But then his luck changed. If Joe Howard lived to be eighty-six he would never get another shock like the one he was about to receive.

Stepping into the glow of the small fire was none

other than the Apache Chief Keoni. There was enough light from the fire for Joe to see that he was dressed pretty much the same way he'd been when he'd last seen him.

He wore a red shirt over black pants with a leather thong belt around his waist. The moccasin boots were laced up around the calf and his shoulder-length straight black hair was held back out of his chisled, angular face with a red bandanna. His face still had a hawkish appearance, with its thin nose and wide, deep-set dark brown eyes.

Joe expelled a long breath as he relaxed back against the tree and lowered the rifle just enough so that he didn't appear threatening. He still had the Indian covered though.

"Chief, what in the world are you doing out here in the night?" Joe asked, stepping over to the fire. Joe had always thought, because he'd always heard, the Indians were afraid to travel at night, because in the event that they died, their spirits couldn't find where to go. Apparently that was wrong in this case.

Keoni stepped closer to the fire as Joe pitched another small limb on it to give more light. Joe felt like a complete fool when he heard additional sounds and saw three braves walk up from three different directions. They each carried Henry repeating rifles. They had walked so quietly that Joe had heard only Keoni. But Keoni was the only one they had wanted Joe to hear. Joe rested the Winchester stock on the tip of his boot and curled his fingers around the barrel.

There was a tiny smile on the chief's mouth and a steady gleam in the dark eyes. If it had been in the

Indian's nature, Joe knew that the chief would have laughed at him.

"We went to fort to meet up with you," Keoni said, dropping down into a squat across the fire from Joe and watching him intently. "But you already gone. Colonel McRaney say you are going to find out why we are getting bad meat from government. Can you get us good meat like white chief promise us?"

Joe thought about all the promises that the white chiefs had made the Indians over the past years and wished that he had a dollar for every promise made and every promise broken. He knew if that could be the case, he'd have more money in his pocket than twenty dollars and wouldn't have to work for a long time.

"I can do that?" Joe replied, feeling a grin pulling at his mouth. "Just as sure as I can ride the moon south." There was sarcasm in his voice. Somehow this Indian had gotten the idea that Joe Howard could make everything all right just by riding into Marathon.

Joe had never known Keoni, or any other Indian for that matter, to be much for facial expressions but he was shocked nearly out of his boots when a deep frown pulled lines between Keoni's black brows.

"What does that mean?" Keoni asked, leaning closer for a better look at Joe. The army scout knew that the metaphor would be hard to explain and wished that he'd used some other example.

"It means that I'm going to do my best to get you good meat," Joe finally said, smiling and shaking his head quickly. "Now, I've got a question for you.

22

What are you all"—he turned and looked at the other three Indians—"doing out here after dark? I didn't think that Indians moved around much in the night."

Before Keoni answered, he looked at each of the three braves, then slowly back to Joe. "We knew that we had nothing to fear from you. We are this many." He held up four long fingers. "You are this many." He dropped three fingers to leave one standing alone. His meaning was perfectly clear. Joe nodded his head slowly. There was no doubt in the Indian's meaning. They could have killed him long before he could have gotten Keoni. They could have gotten him first anyway because they had seen him sitting in the light a long time before he heard them. Joe envied their ability to move in the darkness without being heard. He would probably have been like a cow in a closet if he'd tried to move like that.

Joe felt stupid remembering that he'd told them he was going to count to three before opening fire on them. They probably thought that that was as high as he could count. Joe shivered when he realized that if the Indians had wanted to, they could have killed him where he sat. If they had been savages, as Titus Upshaw had suggested, they probably would have done just that.

But then he took comfort in the fact and relaxed a little when he told himself that Chief Keoni and his men already knew who he was and would let themselves be known before opening fire on him. Being pretty sure that the Indians didn't drink coffee, Joe didn't feel too bad in not having any more to offer them.

"Why did you want to see me?" Joe asked, dropping down on the ground and leaning back against the saddle. He wondered if the four men were planning on going to Marathon with him. Somehow he didn't think that would be such a good idea. He knew that he couldn't do his job with four Indians looking over his shoulder.

"Colonel McRaney say that you left fort before telling him what you plan to do," Keoni answered. Joe could see expectation in the man's dark eyes as if he believed that a plan would jump right out of Joe's mouth and land in front of him.

"I plan to find out why the cattle aren't driven to your camp," Joe answered, looking Keoni straight in the eye. He had learned from past experience in talking with this man to never let his eyes waver. To the Indian that was a positive sign of insincerity. "Couldn't you use the cow hides for moccasins and other things? Couldn't you use other parts for various things?"

Keoni was quick to nod his head and Joe knew from the intensity in his eyes that Keoni was thinking the same thing he was.

"When was the last time you got a wagon load of meat?" Joe asked, stretching his legs out in front of him. Keoni, probably feeling more comfortable now, sat down on the ground and criss-crossed his legs.

"Two moons ago," Keoni answered, holding up two fingers and then making a circle with both hands.

"How often were you told that you would get

24

meat?" Joe asked, knowing that he wasn't going to like what he heard.

"Senator Powers say we would get meat every three moons," Keoni said slowly, disgust edging his voice as he held up three fingers and again made a circle with his hands.

Joe had dealt enough with the Indians to know that they considered a moon to be a month from one phase of the moon around to that same phase again. Two months was a long time to go without meat if half of what they were getting was bad.

"How soon do you think you will know something?" Keoni asked, standing up and looking down at the army scout. His appearance was formidable, and the army scout was suddenly glad that they were both on the same side. He would hate to have this Indian as his adversary. "My people are getting hungry." Joe thought that he detected a slight threat in the Indian's voice.

"I should know something as soon as I get to Marathon in the morning and do some checking," Joe answered, rising to his feet. He suspected that the Indians might be getting hungry not just for meat, but also for a fight.

"Will you come back to fort and tell Colonel McRaney?" Keoni asked, his dark eyes boring into Joe, "Or will you send word on wire?" Joe knew that the chief was talking about him sending McRaney a telegram.

McRaney would probably have gotten a good laugh hearing Keoni asking all these questions. He was beginning to sound like Joe. McRaney would probably swear that they were related.

"It will probably be a waste of time and energy to go straight back to the fort," Joe answered, trying hard not to laugh at Keoni. The Indian had a lot on his mind and hungry people really weren't a laughing matter. "I'll send McRaney a telegram—word on wire—when I hear something. If that is possible." Joe didn't want to promise this demanding Indian something he might not be able to follow through on.

That seemed to satisfy Keoni, and Joe wasn't surprised when the chief extended his hand for a shake.

"I trust you, Joe Howard," Keoni said, gripping Joe's hand firmly and looking him squarely in the eye. "Too bad all white men not like you and Colonel McRaney."

Titus Upshaw suddenly popped into Joe's thoughts and he had to ask, "Do you know Titus Upshaw at the general store in Fort Davis?"

The man's name got Keoni's attention faster than Joe had expected. Keoni had turned to walk away but jerked back around, a slight frown on his bronze face.

"Yes," Keoni answered sharply, folding his arms across his chest as if forming some sort of barricade between him and some unseen force. "He not good man. Not like you and McRaney. Not like Indians."

From the cold tone of Keoni's voice and hostile glare in his eyes, Joe didn't see a need to press the matter any further. He would ask McRaney about it when he got back to the fort.

"I hope it not long before you send word," Keoni

said, his features softening a little. He disappeared into the darkness and Joe wasn't really aware that he was gone until he realized that he was standing alone by the fire. It suddenly dawned on Joe that the other three Indians had already left without his being aware that they were gone.

Joe Howard sat back down and leaned against the saddle there in the darkness, listening to the popping sounds of the dying embers. For a while, he thought he'd dreamed the entire conversation with the Indians. They had come and gone so silently that it was hard to believe that a human could move with so little noise. But as sure as the sun came up in the morning, he was certain there would be some definite signs that the four men had been there.

Joe untied his bedroll, pushed it out, and moved over on it. With so much on his mind, he was afraid he wouldn't be able to sleep a wink. But the last thing he remembered after pulling the blanket up over his shoulders was hearing all the night sounds blending together once again.

A gray haze hung over the mountains and desert when Joe awoke the next morning. A cool breeze nipped at his skin through the blue shirt and he shivered. He wished he'd brought his light jacket but knew that things would warm up some as soon as the sun broke through the clouds.

He was in a hurry to get to Marathon but the rumbling in his stomach made him take enough time to cut off several pieces of salt meat and make flat bread. This he washed down with two cups of strong black coffee. Before he sand-cleaned the frying pan, he poured some water in it for Serge to drink.

"I'll try to find a stream next time, Serge," Joe said, tightening the cinch around the horse, who was tossing his proud head up and down.

After he'd saddled Serge and tied on the bedroll and grub sack, Joe remembered promising himself to look around for sure signs that Chief Keoni and his three silent braves had been there last night.

Joe had been positive there would be footprints and hoofprints attesting to his conversation with the Indian chief last night.

But he was greatly disappointed after he'd swung up on Serge and ridden a small circle, because he didn't find even a horse dropping. There was no evidence that the four men had been anywhere around. Joe would wonder all the way into Marathon how they'd been able to obliterate their tracks. For all I know, he thought, shivering, they could be following me this very minute. He couldn't help looking back over his shoulder. He wasn't disappointed when he didn't see anyone. But that didn't mean that they weren't there.

Joe kept thinking and hoping that the sun would come out as he rode along, but that didn't happen. In fact, the haze thickened and soon thunder rumbled overhead. It sounded like a cannon going off. Serge had been galloping along and Joe's thoughts were occupied. The unexpected sound startled both man and horse and Joe got a few extra yards out of Serge. A slow drizzle began falling and it didn't take long for his clothes to become soaking wet. Rain dripped from the brim of his hat.

The country had needed a good rain for a long time but why did it have to come now, he wondered irritably, wiping the rain from his face.

Joe was almost to the outskirts of town when he realized that he didn't have a plan for finding out about the bad meat.

Colonel McRaney had said that the cattle were sent from Marathon. But he hadn't said who was in charge. Unless there was a ranch around Marathon that was supplying cattle to the government for the Indians, Joe knew that there would have to be some kind of holding pen for them. That shouldn't be too hard to find. A stock yard had its own distinct way of letting itself be found.

Since there were so many low-hanging clouds, it didn't take long for that to happen. The smell seemed to be strongest as he turned Serge south of town.

The drizzle had begun slacking off and Joe was glad of that as he neared the pens. There were at least five hundred head of cattle in the three pens and a plan began forming in Joe's mind as he removed his hat and slapped it against his leg to send water flying.

He knew that he just couldn't go into the office and accuse anyone of purposefully shipping bad meat to the Indians. He had identification in his pocket that he was an army scout. But that wouldn't do if someone in Marathon was connected with the government and was doing something illegal with the cattle before they were butchered for the Indians. Joe still couldn't understand why the cattle weren't driven to the Indians at Elephant Mountain.

Suddenly Joe remembered something that Chief

29

Keoni had said last night and he pulled Serge to a quick stop. When Joe had asked him how long it had been since his people had gotten any meat, Keoni had said two months. Joe wondered if that two months was past the three months that had been promised. Colonel McRaney had told Joe that the Indians were supposed to get three thousand pounds of meat every three months.

Joe knew that somebody was lying to someone. He knew that Eric McRaney wouldn't lie. He would have no reason to. Joe also knew that an Indian's word was his bond. If these two men weren't lying to him, who was lying to them?

Joe wished that he'd caught this last night and had asked Keoni about it. Oh well, it was too late to worry about that now. He would have to think of something else. Right now, the important thing on his mind was how to find out what was going on with the cattle. And those in the pens had to be the ones he'd come to find.

He looked down at his clothes. They were soaking wet. His wet hair was hanging down in his face. He must look like a regular saddle bum. That gave him an idea. If he looked like a bum, maybe he could act like one. He was confident that the plan that had suddenly taken shape in his mind would be an answer to his problem.

Kneeing Serge in the side, they sloshed through the gray mud until they stopped in front of a long whitewashed building with several horses tied to the hitch rail.

Tying Serge, Joe turned his shirt collar up,

removed his hat, tousled his hair across his face even more, replaced the hat at a cocky angle, and knocked on the door. It was yanked open by a man whose father must have been a black grizzly bear. He was one of the biggest men that Joe Howard had ever seen. He had to have stood at least six and a half feet tall and weighed almost three hundred pounds. Black hair seemed to cover every inch that Joe could see of the man. A thick black beard gave him a wild appearance.

"What do you want?" the man snapped in a deep gravelly voice, his black eyes glaring down at Joe. "Who are you?"

"Well, I was riding through," Joe began lamely, arching his brows and shrugging his shoulders as his mind raced to come up with a plausible reason for being there. "I saw all those cows in the pens"—he motioned toward the pens with a wave of his hand— "and thought there might be a job for me. I could really use one."

"We don't need anybody," the big man said, and started to close the door in Joe's face when a voice called out.

"Who is it, Graff?" the deep voice asked in an irritated tone.

"Oh, just some saddle bum looking for a job, Mr. Haverty," Graff replied, a snide grin pulling at his thick lips surrounded by the black beard and mustache. He started to close the door again.

"Wait a minute," the voice belonging to Haverty called out again. "Let him come in. We might be able to use him. We are short-handed."

31

Joe saw disappointment darken Graff's bearded face and knew immediately that if he got into any kind of trouble here, no doubt Graff would be in the middle of it. Graff opened the door wider to allow Joe to come in.

Three other men were in the long room when Graff stepped aside and Joe entered the room. He assumed that the man sitting behind the small, cluttered desk with a chip of wood under one of the legs to level it would be a big man, judging from the strong voice he'd heard. But the man sitting behind the desk wasn't the kind whom Joe would have guessed to be in charge of anything. He just didn't have the appearance of any kind of authority.

Joe had thought at first that the man was sitting down behind the desk. But after looking closer, he saw that he was standing up behind the desk. Joe could tell that Mr. Haverty was just barely five feet tall. The thick hair on his small head was a light yellow, almost a butter color, and his small beady eyes were brown with green flecks around the edges. He probably weighed a little over a hundred pounds. He reminded Joe of a small, beady-eyed brown lizard. Haverty was immaculately dressed in a tan suit, light brown shirt, and dark brown tie.

"I'm Winston Haverty," the little man said, giving Joe a once-over. "You say you need a job, huh?" The man's deep voice belied his height and it was all that Joe could do not to laugh at him.

"Yeah," Joe answered, nodding and hooking his thumbs over his belt. "It's been a good while since I've had two nickels to rub together. So how about it?

Do you think you can use me? I really need a job. I've worked with cattle before."

Joe watched Graff and Haverty exchange knowing looks. He felt a knot pull in his stomach when Haverty switched his gaze from Graff down to the Colt .45 tied down to Joe's leg.

"Do you know how to use that thing?" Haverty asked pointedly, narrowing his brown eyes as a speculating smile slid across his thin face.

"Well," Joe said offhandedly, drawing his mouth to one side and arching his brows, a gleam in his eyes. "I've been known to bring down a rabbit or two." There was a warning deep in his eyes that dared Haverty or the big man Graff to argue with him about his ability with the gun.

"Where was your last job?" Graff asked, walking over to the desk and dropping down on the corner. Joe was surprised that it didn't break under the man's ponderous weight. The Joslyn .44 where Graff rested his ham-sized right hand looked like a child's toy.

Joe felt as if he were being picked clean by the two men as they watched and questioned him, and he knew that it wouldn't matter what answer he gave. They would either hire him or make him leave. So he didn't say anything.

"All right," Haverty said, expelling a deep breath and shaking his head at Graff. "It doesn't matter what his last job was. We need an extra hand since Newsome left. We've got to move those cattle tomorrow."

Joe felt a little better since it hadn't taken much time and effort to find the cattle and the men. Now all he had to do was find out what the men were doing with the meat that caused it to spoil before it got to the Indians.

"Be here at sunup in the morning," Graff said curtly, sitting down behind the desk. He had to sit on the edge of the chair so that his feet would touch the floor. "We've got a lot of work to do."

Once again Joe wanted to laugh at Winston Haverty. He looked like a little kid sitting there trying to play grown-up. But no matter how small Haverty was and how big Graff was, the little man wasn't afraid of him. The Colt .38 on the desk by Haverty's right hand probably made him Graff's equal.

Turning to leave, Joe wondered if it was Haverty's idea to give the Indians bad meat, or was he only a spoke in the wheel?

Chapter 2

Joe backed out the door, keeping a wary eye on Graff. The mountain of a man had seemed to take an instant dislike against Joe and the army scout knew that it wouldn't take much for him to go at him. He swung up on Serge and rode at a fast gallop back toward town. He was pretty sure that the cattle in the pens were the ones that were supposed to go to Chief Keoni. Joe was amazed at how easy it had been to get a job with so few questions asked.

Apparently Winston Haverty and Graff had really thought, and there was no reason for them to do otherwise, that he was a saddle bum and looking for a job. He must have looked pretty bad. He was glad now that he hadn't shaved before leaving the fort.

Joe guessed that the reason that Haverty had told him to come back at such an early hour in the morning was that some of the cattle were to be butchered or he wanted to get an early start in driving them somewhere. He wished that he'd had more time to look at the cattle and see what kind of condition they were in. Maybe Haverty and his bunch were buying two kinds of cattle. Good quality for themselves and an inferior quality for the Indians.

But wait a minute, Joe thought pulling Serge to a stop in front of a two-story wooden building with the word HOTEL painted in black letters on it. Just because Winston Haverty had the cattle didn't mean that he was doing anything illegal. Maybe he was a private owner and the government bought the cattle from him for the Indians. There had been nothing in the sparsely furnished office to indicate that anything military was involved.

Other than the lopsided desk and chair in the office, there had only been a square wood-burning stove, a coat rack, two more chairs, and a wooden bench that would sit perhaps three people. A wooden filing cabinet looked lost at the end of the room.

Joe dismounted, tied Serge to the rickety hitching rail in front of the hotel, and went in. A tall, robust, black-haired woman was sitting behind a counter. She looked up from a newspaper with a disinterested expression on her oval face when Joe walked in. The look changed in her dark eyes as she ran them up and down his untidy but lean body and a slow smile pulled at her wide red mouth. She was one of the prettiest women Joe had seen in a long time.

"Well, good looking," she said, putting the paper down and cupping her chin in her upturned palm, "you must have had a bath with all of your clothes on. How about a nice bath and room." Joe was sure

36

there was a double meaning in her offer and he felt his face getting warm at the woman's close scrutiny. He'd seen a hound dog look at a bone like that one time just before the dog jumped on it with all four feet.

"You're half right," Joe said, shifting his weight from one foot to the other as he usually did when he was uncomfortable or embarrassed. He'd known his share of women but he usually made the first move. "I was caught out in the rain and I could use a bath and a room. Do you have a vacancy? It's been a long day."

The woman ran her dark eyes slowly up and down him again as she reached behind her and took a key from one of the wooden pegs on the wall and handed it to him.

"Sugar, if I didn't have an extra room," she said, lowering her lashes and smiling suggestively at him, "you could stay with me. Maybe I should take the key back. What do you say?"

Joe knew she was joking, or he wanted to believe that she was joking and that she would probably have said the same thing to Colonel Eric McRaney if he'd been standing there.

"Maybe later," Joe said, winking at her. As he started up the stairs to the second floor, Joe remembered that he'd left his saddlebags and bedroll tied on Serge. The horse would have to be stabled, too. He'd been so astonished at this impudent woman that he'd forgotten about the black horse outside.

The rain had stopped and everything smelled good

37

and fresh when Joe went back downstairs and outside. Glancing down the street, he saw the livery not too far away. Untying Serge, they sloshed through the gray muddy street.

"I'll bet you're hungry enough to eat a whole bucket of oats, huh?" Joe said, walking close to the big black horse. As if understanding exactly what Joe had said to him, the horse nodded his head up and down and rubbed his jaw against Joe's shoulder. "You need a good rubdown, too," Joe said, reaching out and rubbing the animal's forehead. "I wonder how much it would take for me to get a rubdown at the hotel?" Joe mused out loud. "Probably not much, judging from the look in that woman's eyes."

"Ya, and vot kin I do for you," a middle-aged man of medium build and height asked Joe. The army scout did a double-take first at the man's accent and second when he looked at the man's head. It was covered with the strangest color of hair that Joe had ever seen. It wasn't white or gray like that of an older person. It wasn't blond and it wasn't a light brown. It was a mixture of all the colors, if that was possible. Somewhere down the line there had to have been some red because there was a pink tinge to the hair also. The man's skin would have been fair if he hadn't been out in the hot, arid west Texas sun. His cheeks looked like two cherry red tomatoes. He appeared to be a man of good disposition or that was the way Joe judged him from the twinkling dark blue eyes deep-set under light brown brows that peaked in the middle. Not only had the man's hair gotten Joe's attention, but his accent rang unfamiliar in his ears.

38

It wasn't Spanish, it wasn't from England, and it wasn't Irish.

But that really shouldn't have been anything really strange. The West was fast becoming a melting pot for accents, customs, and skin color. Everyone was coming West for any number of reasons: not enough room in the East. To escape the ravages of the war. To find gold in the West. To get away from the law. That meant that the migrants would have to have homes and that meant that someone or something would have to give. And it wouldn't take a genius to figure out who would have to do the giving because the Indian had always given a lot and had received very little or nothing, in most cases, at all in return.

The Indians were being called savages by people like Titus Upshaw because they were trying to hang on to and protect their families and land. Nobody in their right mind, Joe Howard included, would stand by and allow strangers to try to come into their homes and take over.

Joe must have been staring at the man as those thoughts ran through his mind because a worried frown marred the man's otherwise smooth forehead.

"Mister, are ya all right?" the man asked, his eyes narrowing in concern as he looked up at Joe. He reached out and touched Joe's arm.

"Oh, yeah," Joe said, jerking his head sharply to clear his mind. "I was just thinking. Old Serge here is so hungry that he's beginning to look at my hat. If you have time, he might even like a good rubdown. I've been so busy lately that I haven't had time to do it. He likes to be rubbed between his ears."

"Don't vorry yourself about it," the livery man said, reaching out and taking Serge's reins from Joe. "My name is Iggy Jennssen and I will take good care of the old boy."

For some reason Joe wasn't surprised by the man's given name. After the strange accent and the odd-colored hair, there wasn't much left about the man to surprise him.

Joe took his bedroll and saddlebags from the horse and turned to walk away but stopped when he heard Jennssen call out, "Young fella. Don't ye vant yer long gun?"

Shaking his head in amusement at Jennssen's strange description for the Winchester, Joe walked back to the livery. Serge was already inside chomping on a bucket of oats and Joe couldn't believe his eyes when he walked in. Hanging on the sides of four stalls were McClellan saddles. He started to 'walk over to the horse for a closer look at the saddles but didn't want to make Jennssen suspicious of him. Pulling the Winchester from the scabbard, he nodded to Jennssen and started back up the street to the hotel. His mind was in a jumble of questions.

Why were there four McClellan saddles at the livery? They had to be for the four horses in the stalls. Why were four soldiers here in Marathon? Joe wondered. Soldiers were the only ones who would have a valid reason to use a military saddle. It had been constructed for convenience and light weight with no pommel and narrow leather for the iron stirrups. Civilians usually preferred the common saddle.

He knew that there were no soldiers this far from Fort Davis, or at least there weren't supposed to be. Joe had never made it his business to keep tabs on all the men because, for one thing, there were too many of them and, for another, they weren't that much his concern. But Marathon was too far away for any of the soldiers to ride from Fort Davis for any kind of entertainment. Then a thought struck him and he got an entirely different perspective on the whole situation. Maybe someone just liked to use the lighter weight military saddle as opposed to the heavier Western saddle.

Now if you believe that, Joe scoffed to himself as he went back up the street to the hotel, you'll believe that Chief Keoni and Colonel Eric McRaney will change places next Thursday. One person with a McClellan saddle, maybe. But four McClellan saddles at the same time and at the same place? Not hardly.

Joe breathed a sigh of relief when he went into the hotel and saw that Miss Hot Lashes wasn't behind the counter. Going up the stairs, he opened the door to the meagerly furnished room, tossed the saddlebags and bedroll down on the bed, and leaned the Winchester against the wall at the head of the bed. Feeling like the dirty saddle bum that Graff had called him earlier, Joe took clean clothes from the saddlebags and went back downstairs. This time his luck ran out. Seeing the flirtatious woman sitting behind the desk, Joe realized that she hadn't been at the hotel when he'd arrived and that was how he'd gotten up to his room so easily.

."Ma'am, is there a bath house out back?" he asked, knowing that he was letting himself in for more advances and suggestions. Joe knew that she had been joking and if he hadn't had more important things on his mind, he might not be so hasty in ignoring her attention. He smiled to himself as he wondered what she would do if he turned the tables on her.

Her olive skin was smooth over high cheekbones and she knew how to use rouge and eye kohl without looking like a cheap hussy. Brows as black as her hair and lashes gave her a slight gypsy appearance by the way they arched up over her eyes. A full red mouth, which could probably make a lot of men's dreams come true, seemed always to be smiling.

"I haven't been called ma'am since I was . . ." she began, and snapped her mouth shut on the last word. "My name is Saber Entonelli." She pressed her lips into a tight line so she wouldn't laugh when his eyes widened. "Most people just call me Saber," she said, batting her dark brown eyes rapidly a couple of times and nodding as she drew the word out slowly.

"I can see why," Joe said before thinking. "Sorry," he apologized quickly. "About the bath house," he continued, smiling sheepishly at her and bracing himself for what he knew would follow the question.

"Yes, there's a bath house out back, if you want to call it that," Saber said with a smile, dropping her chin into her palm on an upraised elbow. "You could get a much better bath in my room," she suggested, running the tip of her tongue around the edge of her mouth.

"And just how could that be possible?" Joe asked, deciding to join in on her little game for a while. He knew that she was probably just saying these things to pass the time out here in the middle of nowhere.

"Because, sugar," she replied softly, lowering her thick lashes and leaning across the counter toward him, "I would bathe you myself. You would think that you had died and gone straight up to those pearly gates." She held Joe's gaze for a few seconds and he could see the beginning of a twinkle deep in her dark eyes and tugging at the edges of her mouth. He knew that she wanted to laugh as much as he did. There was no seriousness in her eyes and he realized that she would probably have said the same thing to U. S. Grant if he'd been standing there. She was just making conversation.

"You're probably right," Joe said, letting his mouth slide into a smile, "and I'll probably hate myself for turning you down right now. But I want to get a simple hot bath, eat a big meal, and get a good night's sleep before I start on my new job tomorrow. Something tells me that if you gave me a bath, eating and sleeping would be the last thing I would do afterward."

Saber Entonelli's eyes flew wide open and her red mouth gaped as a blush raced up her face and into her hair line. She shook her head quickly and took a deep breath.

"New job?" she repeated skeptically, pulling her chin down as he started toward the door. "Here in Marathon? Doing what?" All joking, suggestions, and innuendos were gone and only genuine interest and sarcasm were in her eyes and voice now.

"Yeah," Joe answered, a little surprised by the look in her eyes, "here in Marathon. I don't know what I'll be doing but I'll be working for Winston Haverty down at those cattle pens." He waved his arm in that direction. Saber Entonelli's dark eyes flew wide open and her mouth gaped open big enough to put a fist in.

"Mister"—she paused long enough to look down at the last entry in the register book—"Howard, not only do you need a good bath, but you also need someone to look at your head. I don't think you have everything that you need in there."

Joe felt the hair on the back of his neck stand up straight, and he knew by her perplexed expression that she wasn't kidding.

"Why?" Joe asked doubtfully, walking back to the counter, a deep frown on his tanned and stubbled face. "Winston Haverty seemed nice enough to me. What's wrong with him? How well do you know him?"

"Well," Saber began slowly, pursing her lips tightly and folding her arms under her ample breast, "I don't want to get into something that's none of my business and I don't begrudge anybody getting a job in this day and age. But I would suggest that you watch your step and your back." She stopped for a second, took a deep breath, and seemed to give careful consideration to what she was going to say. "Especially if you're working with Bernie Graff."

Joe looked down at the floor, slowly raised his eyes to meet Saber's mystified gaze, then threw back his

44

head and roared in laughter. He couldn't help it. The name "Bernie" just didn't fit the bear of a man. He should have been named Luke or Jake or at least John. But not Bernie.

Realizing that he was the only one laughing, Joe composed himself, cleared his throat, and coughed. "I don't suppose you're going to tell me why I should watch out for Ber—" He just couldn't say the name. "For Graff, are you?" Joe was glad that she just shook her head. He knew that if he'd had to wait for a vocal answer to his question, he'd burst out laughing again.

Turning around, he opened the door, went down the hall, outside to an adobe building with the word BATHS painted across the front in red paint, and went in. He'd used the phrase "hot bath" just to make himself feel better, but when he stepped inside the bath house, he knew that wasn't going to happen. He'd meant a hot water bath. A hundred-gallon wooden keg stood in the center of the room where five cubicles were divided by thin pieces of wood with a three-foot door about two feet from the ceiling and floor to give privacy. Two galvanized and dented tubs leaned against the keg. Dingy towels and yellow bars of soap were on a small table in front of the keg.

Lifting the wooden lid, Joe was pleased to see that the keg was almost full. But he was a little disgusted at the slight stale odor. It was hard to tell how long the water had been there.

But in any case, he needed a bath. The old water couldn't make him smell any worse than his sweaty and still damp clothes already did. Slinging a towel over his shoulder and putting a bar of soap in his shirt pocket, Joe poured one of the tubs half full of water and pulled it inside the cubicle.

Joe stripped down, poured a dipper of water over himself, and lathered up all over. The soap had a nice fragrance. He had bathed with some soaps that smelled like horse liniments. While he washed his hair, rinsed off, and dried, he thought about what Saber Entonelli had said about Bernie Graff.

Had she been comparing his size to that of the big man? Is that why she had been so quick with her caution and then refused to say any more to explain it? Joe just hoped he would never have to go up against the big man in any physical confrontation. That would be like a cat playing with a cougar! There was no doubt about who would lose.

The clean clothes felt good and he smelled much better. The water hadn't been that stale and the soap helped a lot. But something told him that if he was going to be butchering cattle for Winston Haverty tomorrow, he would smell much worse than he did today. Joe knew that that job would probably fall to him since a new man usually got the dirty work.

Gathering up his dirty clothes, Joe went back to the hotel. He'd noticed a sign in the corner of the lobby for dirty clothes to be washed. Paper sacks were stacked under the sign. Joe put his clothes in a sack and wrote his name on it. A rumbling in his stomach made him aware that he hadn't eaten since early that morning. There was no dining room at the hotel but he'd noticed a café two doors away. The summer sun was bearing down on the street, and the heat steamed up from the damp ground and slapped him in the face as he walked toward the café. A black dog that hadn't missed any meals and was a welcome mat for fleas stopped in the middle of the street to scratch behind his ear.

The searing heat was probably the reason why so few people were in the stiflingly hot place. Even though the ceiling was high and the windows were open on all three sides, there didn't seem to be a free breath of air to mingle in with the aroma of food and coffee.

But no matter how hot it was in the place, Joe's taste buds were assaulted by the aromas and he knew that he would probably die of malnutrition before his well-done steak, fried potatoes, and cornbread were set down in front of him. His plate would hardly need to be washed when he finished eating.

"You must have been empty all the way down to your toes," the tall, slender, redheaded youngster said as he filled Joe's cup for the third time with the strongest coffee Joe had ever tasted. It could stand almost by itself.

"Yeah," Joe answered, grinning up at him, "and I'll take a slice of whatever kind of pie you've got."

Joe regretted the order because whoever had made the apple pie wasn't aware that some liquid should have been added. It was mostly sliced apples and crust. But it was filling, and it satisfied his sweet tooth for a while.

Joe stood up, paid for the meal, and was going out the door when Bernie Graff and another man who'd been in the office at the cattle pens walked in. When

Graff saw Joe, he shot him a contemptuous glare.

"I hope you'll be able to hold up your end of the work tomorrow," Graff said snidely, frowning belligerently down at Joe, raw dislike in his black eyes. "Me and Jack Lucas here don't need no help."

"It will depend on what Mr. Haverty tells me to do," Joe retaliated, arching his brows and dropping his hand down to the handle of the Colt .45 tied to his right leg. "If I can't hold up my end of the work, then I'll just tell Mr. Haverty and ride on."

A small bell rang in the back of Joe Howard's mind and told him that Bernie Graff wasn't used to having anyone, especially someone smaller than he was, talk back to him the way that Joe had just done.

The big man pressed his thick lips together tightly and the nostrils in his flat nose flared. Joe guessed from the looks of the lopsided nose that Graff had been in at least one fight. The hump across the bridge indicated that it had been broken. If a man had done it with his fist, Joe would almost give a month's pay to see what that man looked like.

"Just don't get in my way," Graff warned sarcastically, pushing past Joe into the café. Joe heard Jack Lucas expel a long breath as he walked by him.

Since he didn't have anything else to do until morning, Joe decided to go down to the livery and give Serge a good rubdown. Iggy Jennssen had said that he would do it, but maybe he wouldn't have the time. Maybe Joe could find out something about those horses with the McClellan saddles. His gut feeling told him that there had to be some soldiers connected with them. He wished that he'd asked Saber if she knew anything about soldiers being in town.

Joe suspected that since Winston Haverty had been so quick to hire him, and with so many cattle in the pens, that the cattle were either going to be driven someplace or the butchering would start early in the morning.

As soon as Serge caught a glimpse of Joe, the big black horse began nodding his head up and down and rumbling low in his throat.

"Dot is von great horse ye've got there," Iggy Jennssen said in the strange accent, pushing his odd-colored hair back out of his face. His dark blue eyes twinkled in admiration.

"Yeah, I kind of like the old nag," Joe said, picking up the long currycomb and walking over to the horse. Serge rubbed his head against Joe's shoulder as Joe began brushing the long smooth neck.

"Are ye just passing through?" Jennssen asked, dropping down on an upturned wooden bucket and crossing his legs.

"I was," Joe answered, deciding to still play it cautiously with the seemingly overfriendly man. Joe took a quick glance around the livery and saw that theré was enough work to keep a man busy all day. Two of the stalls opposite him needed to be raked out. A buggy, with the front left axle propped up on a block of wood, had a broken wheel leaning against it, and the water bucket by the door was almost empty. Either the man was lazy or spent his time doing other things.

Joe could tell from the expectant look on the man's red face that he was more interested in what he was going to tell him than getting the work done.

"I'd thought about going up to Pecos," Joe went on, giving Serge long, deep strokes with the comb. "I was going to spend the night here and head up that way when I saw all those cattle in the pens. I went by, asked a man named Winston Haverty for a job, and I start to work for him in the morning."

The anticipating expression changed on Iggy Jennssen's face as fast as the joking expression had changed on Saber Entonelli's. Joe had been watching Jennssen from the corner of his eye and was only a little surprised by what he saw. A mask of stillness slid across Jennssen's features and he stared down at the ground between his run-down boots for a long time before saying anything. Suddenly he was seized by a coughing fit and stood up.

"Are you all right?" Joe asked, hoping that he put enough concern in his voice. He knew full well that Winston Haverty's name was what had caused the attack. Joe wondered what kind of hold the little yellow-haired man had on at least two people in town. "Is something wrong?"

"My young friend," Jennssen said resolutely, clearing his throat, then drawing in a long, slow breath. "It is not my place to be telling you vot to do. But if I ver you, I vould give a little more thought to going on up to Pecos. You might find a better job up there."

"Why?" Joe asked, resting both arms on Serge's

50

back and frowning deeply at Jennssen. All of the friendly inquisitiveness had disappeared from the man's blue eyes and he seemed uneasy. He appeared nervous now as he scratched the strange-colored hair on his head. Joe was beginning to realize that Winston Haverty really did have some kind of hold or power on a few people here in Marathon. He wondered what kind of reaction the waiter at the café would have had if Joe had told him about his job with Haverty or Graff.

Maybe Winston Haverty owned all the businesses in town and each employee was afraid of losing his job when a stranger rode into town and would probably work for less money.

Jennssen started to take another breath to say something but was stopped by footsteps crunching on the ground outside. He snapped his mouth shut on whatever he was about to say when Bernie Graff and Jack Lucas came into the livery. The big man's shadow filled the entire door.

"Now ain't this just dandy?" Graff stated more than asked when he saw Joe with the comb in his hand. "I only laid eyes on you for the first time early this morning and so far you've managed to be everywhere that I've gone." Dislike was rampant in the big man's black eyes and he shook his head in disgust.

"It does seem to be a small place, doesn't it?" Joe said contritely, holding the comb in both hands to keep his right hand up and away from the Colt .45. For some reason Joe knew it wouldn't take much provocation for Bernie Graff to come at him. Joe wasn't aware that a small grin had pulled at the corner of his mouth until he saw blinding rage darken Graff's eyes even more, if that was possible.

"Just what are you laughing at?" Graff bellowed, his loud voice bouncing off the walls as he took a menacing step toward Joe. "What's so danged funny?"

Joe felt his heart slam against his ribs and began beating faster. He'd never felt so threatened in all his life. He could almost feel his life oozing out of every pore in his body. His mouth felt dry when he swallowed.

"Ah, Graff," Jack Lucas chided, reaching out and taking the big man by the arm. "He didn't mean anything. Let it go."

God, I hope he does let it go—whatever it is, Joe prayed silently, suddenly feeling cold all over. The very thing that had crossed his mind in the café only a few moments ago was about to come true. He was going to have to defend himself against this bear of a man who would almost make two of him.

"I want to know what he was laughing at," Graff insisted, pulling his arm free with a vicious jerk. "He was looking at me, so he had to be laughing at me and I want to know what it was."

Before Joe Howard knew what was happening, Bernie Graff reached out, grabbed a handful of his shirt and that was just about the entire front, almost lifted him up off the ground, and jerked Joe toward him.

"Nobody laughs at me," Graff snarled, his thick lips turned in against his square short teeth. "Do you understand? Nobody!'' To give emphasis to the warning, although that really wasn't necessary because Graff had already gotten Joe's undivided attention from the second that he had walked into the livery, he gave Joe a quick shake. In Joe's mind he could see a little kitten in a cougar's mouth.

Joe felt as if his head was about to snap off. If he didn't do something fast, this big man could kill him.

But what could he do short of shooting Graff? It would be a waste to try using his fists against the man. Divine intervention had been put to the test for the past twenty-three years, taking care of Joe Howard. And the job wasn't finished yet. Joe didn't want to pull the .45 and shoot Graff. That would be murder. Pure and simple. But that would be no different from what Graff was about to do to him. The big man drew back his right fist and popped Joe squarely in the face. Joe had more or less anticipated such a move and jerked his head back. But Graff's fist was almost as big as Joe's face and the blow caught him on the mouth and chin. Joe tasted blood as his teeth cut into his mouth.

Joe still held the currycomb in his right hand, the metal teeth pointing outward. Bringing his arm up, although there wasn't a lot of room to move, Joe bashed the comb as hard as he could against the left side of Graff's bearded face. With a yell of pain and a curse in rage, Graff let go of Joe's shirt and slapped his left hand up against his cheek. Blood was on his hand from the tiny puncture wounds.

Dropping the comb, Joe jerked the Colt .45 from

the holster as he stumbled backward and landed against one of the stall doors. He thumbed the trigger back and knew that that was all that had stopped Graff from rushing at him. Rage, pain, and hate were alive in Graff's bulging black eyes. Jack Lucas and Iggy Jennssen had made no move to take sides even though the odds were against Joe.

"What in the devil is going on here?" a deep voice called out from the livery door. Joe shifted his eyes just enough away from Graff, who was looking at the blood on his hand, to see Winston Haverty standing there with the other man who'd been in the office earlier that morning. There was shock all over Haverty's small, tanned face as he glanced rapidly from Graff to Joe and back to Graff.

"Graff, do you always have to get into trouble every time that I send you to do something?" Irritation snapped in Haverty's brown eyes and pulled a deep frown between his brows.

"This low-down saddle bum laughed at me," the big man whined. He sounded like a spanked baby and even had a pout on his thick mouth.

Haverty stared at Graff, letting his jaw drop a fraction. He shifted his gaze down to the ground, then slowly raised it up to look at Graff again. All the while Haverty shook his head slowly. He batted his eyes rapidly.

"You beat all, you know that, Graff," Haverty said, hooking his thumbs over the expensive leather belt around his middle that even at his height had a little thickness to it. "Howard, put the gun away. Graff, hasn't anyone ever laughed at you before?"

"Yeah, but not a total stranger," Graff replied, ducking his head and looking embarrassed.

Joe wasn't sure how to judge this big man standing there with four pairs of eyes riveted on him. He was big enough to handle himself in any kind of physical situation but he couldn't cope with anything mental. That might work to Joe's advantage later.

"Mr. Howard," Haverty said wearily, expelling a long, deep breath, a minute grin on his small face, "will you please tell Mr. Graff why you were laughing at him, if indeed you were."

Joe thought for a second about what the consequences could be if he answered Haverty's question truthfully. But decided that he couldn't be in any more trouble with Graff than he already was. Total dislike was written all over the big man's bearded face.

"Well," Joe began, taking a deep breath before swallowing hard and shifting his weight from one foot to the other. He decided to tell the truth. Maybe Winston Haverty wouldn't let Graff kill him. "It just struck me as funny that a man as big and able-bodied as Graff certainly is would have a first name like Bernie." Joe's voice cracked on the name in spite of all he could do to stop it.

A silence hung over the livery as the four men still looked at Graff. Joe was soon to learn that Bernie Graff wasn't the mental giant that he'd first suspected him of being at the cattle pens early that morning.

"Well, I've got news for you," Graff said derisively, pulling down the corners of his mouth, "my name really isn't Bernie." He lifted his head smugly. Graff would have been a whole lot better off if he'd just kept his mouth shut and let it go at that. But he didn't. "It's Bernard." Graff seemed certain that the explanation would take care of any more ridicule about his name and dared them to say anything.

The five men looked at Graff, then exchanged amused looks between them. Suddenly the livery was filled with ribald laughter. The sound bounced off the walls and assaulted their ears. Even the horses jumped.

Knowing that he was the butt of their laughter and that Joe had instigated the whole thing, Graff became fire-fighting mad. Joe was positive he could see smoke coming out of Graff's large ears. Graff took a couple of steps toward Joe, and Joe could feel his heart actually skip a few beats. He reached for the pistol handle.

"All right," Winston Haverty called out loudly. "Both of you! That will be enough! You two are going to have to work together for a while and I don't have time to play nursemaid for you two. Neither does Ed Spencer." Haverty jabbed his thumb over his shoulder, indicating the other man standing behind him.

Graff shot Joe a castigating look that would curl a horse's mane.

"Just tell him not to laugh at my name anymore," Graff whined. He still sounded like a little kid.

"Mr. Howard," Haverty said patiently, closing and opening his eyes slowly, "would you please not laugh at his name anymore."

56

"You've got it," Joe answered, pressing his mouth into a firm, thin line so that he wouldn't smile and held Haverty's gaze intently. Surpressed laughter was deep in both men's eyes.

Joe couldn't believe how much Graff's bearing had changed in the past few minutes. But maybe the big man's name was the only sensitive thing about him. Joe would have to think about that later. Right now, he was too busy watching Winston Haverty and Bernie Graff putting the McClellan saddles on two of the horses in the stalls. He wondered about the other two saddles and had the question about one answered when Ed Spencer, walking slowly across the ground, put one of them on a horse and swung up. That still left one more McClellan when Jack Lucas put an ordinary saddle on a horse. He'd soon have that query taken care of. But Bernie Graff got Joe's attention as the big man swung up on a bay mare. Graff's massive bulk almost hid the small military saddle under him and it was all that Joe could do again not to laugh.

"I'll be along in about five minutes, Mr. Haverty," Jennssen said, picking up the extra McClellan and moving it closer to the other horse in the stall. "I'm going to clean up here a little before I leave."

"All right," Haverty replied, swinging up on a buckskin and settling his foot more comfortably in the iron stirrup. As Haverty, Graff, Lucas, and Spencer rode out of the livery, another staggering question pulled a knot in Joe's stomach. If these three horses belonged to the three men who had just left, who owned the other three horses that Joe had seen earlier at the cattle pens?

Joe was glad now that he hadn't told Iggy Jennssen he was an army scout. If Jennssen was working for Winston Haverty and the rest, which obviously he was, Joe's identity was the last thing he needed to know. But Joe wanted to find out about those extra horses. They had to belong to someone. He'd seen three horses there, and up until a few minutes ago, he'd assumed they belonged to Haverty, Graff, and Spencer. But they had left on horses from the livery, and everyone except Jack Lucas was using a McClellan saddle. The question about those saddles was eating a hole in Joe's brain. He'd have to be careful how he phrased the question or he'd make Iggy Jennssen suspicious about him. But Joe Howard had never been known for his patience and diplomacy.

"How many men does Winston Haverty have working for him?" Joe asked nonchalantly, bending down and picking up the currycomb again to start brushing Serge.

"Now dat he's hired you," Jennssen answered, picking up a rake and making a few jabs at the grass in the stall, "he has seven."

That would account for the extra three horses at the pens, Joe mused. But then his thoughts kept nagging at him. Why were Haverty, Graff, Spencer, and apparently Jennssen using McClellan saddles? There was only one sure way to find out.

"Why are you four using that kind of saddle?" Joe asked, pretending to be paying close attention to grooming the black horse. But he raised his head just enough to see Jennssen. Obviously the question didn't bother him because he just kept on with his feeble attempt at the raking.

"They vere gifts," he said candidly, wiping his shirtsleeve across his sweaty forehead.

"Gifts?" Joe blurted out before thinking. He dropped his arm, letting the comb dangle in his hand. Something was wrong here. Those saddles could not have been gifts. The army just did not give away its saddles.

But maybe Jennssen didn't mean gifts in the traditional way. Maybe the soldiers who had used the saddles before hadn't been aware that they were giving away the saddles. Could the four saddles have been gotten in some other way? Were the saddles mixed up in some way with the cattle and Chief Keoni? The one-word reply "yes" surged inside Joe's head.

Joe Howard felt cold all over even though it was blistering hot in the livery, and shivers ran up and down his spine as numerous possibilities flashed through his mind as to how these men could have been the recipients of those saddles.

He walked around to the other side of Serge and began brushing him, wondering where the four men were going and how soon Jennssen would join them. Jennssen seemed to be extra careful as he leaned the rake against the wall and saddled the horse with the other McClellan. Without saying anything or looking at Joe, he swung up on the horse and rode out of the livery, taking off at a fast gallop after the four men. Joe wondered what Jennssen was trying to prove by staying behind and pretending to rake. He certainly hadn't accomplished anything in the short time since the four others had left.

For a split second Joe gave serious thought about riding back to Fort Davis and telling Colonel Eric McRaney what he'd learned. But that would only be a waste of time, and actually when he really thought about it, he hadn't learned all that much. He'd found the cattle. Four men had McClellan saddles. So what? Nothing pointed to anything dishonest yet.

Joe had to satisfy his curious nature and find out about the other three riders. Putting the currycomb down, he filled the water bucket in Serge's stall and stepped out into the hot sunlight. As he walked toward the cattle pens, he wondered why Iggy Jennssen had acted so strangely when he'd told him that he had a job with Haverty. Maybe Jennssen hadn't been aware that Haverty needed anyone else.

There were only two horses tied in front of the building at the cattle pens when Joe walked up. He wondered if the other rider had joined Haverty and the other four men.

Joe stepped up on the porch and knocked on the door. When there was no answer to his knock, he opened the door and peeped in. The room was empty. This time his vision wasn't hampered by the bulk of Graff and he had a better look around.

To his left was a black potbellied stove with a well-used coffeepot on top. Two double bunks were on either side and at the end of the room. Yellow rain slickers were piled on a straight-backed chair in the corner. The bare-topped desk at the opposite end of the room got Joe's attention and he started toward it. But looking out through the window, he saw two men coming and knew he wouldn't have time to search it.

Going out the back door, Joe walked in long strides toward the first pen and leaned his arm across the top post just as he heard a gruff voice call out behind him.

"Who are you?" the medium-sized man asked, picking big square yellow teeth with a match that had been whittled down into a toothpick. The other man, so tall and thin that it wouldn't take much of a breeze to blow him away, made sucking sounds with his tongue against his teeth. Apparently they had just come from the café. "What do you think you're doing here?"

"I'm Joe Howard," Joe answered, hooking his thumbs over his pockets. "I'm supposed to start work here early in the morning, and since there's nothing to do in town except sleep or listen to the wind blow, I thought I'd come down here and try to figure out what's going to happen to these cattle."

Joe glanced noncommittally from the men over to the cattle, then back to the men again. There was nothing suspicious about them. Maybe they just worked here.

"They're all branded," Joe continued, shrugging his shoulders. "Although the brands are different, a running iron could change one brand into another."

Joe noticed that the two men exchanged a quick and surprised look when he mentioned a running iron.

61

"Didn't Mr. Haverty tell you exactly what you'd be doing here?" the tall man asked, frowning skeptically down at Joe.

"No," Joe answered dejectedly, arching his brows and shaking his head slowly.

"Well, we..." the tall man began, but was stopped when his companion caught him by the arm, a warning in his steady gaze.

"Why don't we let Mr. Haverty explain it all to him in the morning?" he said cautiously.

"Yeah, you're probably right," the tall man said, nodding his head rapidly. "I'm Miles Rymer and this is Frank Zahn."

Joe shook hands with the two men and he was a little surprised when they turned and walked back toward the building without any more comment or questions. Of course there wasn't a lot that he could do by himself with that many cattle, but it seemed a little strange to him that they would leave a stranger there by himself.

Since Rymer and Zahn didn't seem too concerned about his being at the pens, Joe decided that now would be a good time to take a look at the cows. All the cattle could have fit into one pen and he wondered why they had been divided into three groups.

At first it didn't dawn on Joe that there was a difference in the cattle in the first pen from those in the second and third pens. It was only when he'd reached the last pen and had turned to start back to the hotel that he realized that the cattle in the first pen were in much better physical shape than those in the second and certainly better than those in the last one. Joe could actually see the ribs, could almost hang his hat on the hip bones, and their hides were dull. They appeared to be standing up only by the aid of a miracle. In contrast, those in the first pen were fat, agile, bright-eyed, and had a shine to their hides.

The cows in the second pen were in much better shape than those in the last pen but not quite the same quality of those in the first.

Joe Howard didn't want to believe what the little voice in the far recesses of his mind was telling him. But like it or not, the fact was as clear as the odd-colored hair on Iggy Jennssen's head. Chief Keoni and his people were getting the cattle that could hardly stand up! The reason that they couldn't stand up was that they were sick. It didn't take two glances to see that. Joe wondered if Haverty and his bunch would throw in one from the middle pen for good measure. He doubted it.

There was one question left to be answered. No, two questions had to be answered. Who was getting the healthy cattle? Were they butchered or sold on the hoof? And where had the four men gotten those McClellan saddles?

Rage shot through Joe as he walked back toward the hotel. He knew that if he had been in the Indian chief's moccasins, he would have broken the agreement with the government long ago if his people were hungry and weren't getting the meat that would have taken care of the problem.

Saber Entonelli was sitting in a wide wicker chair by the window reading a newspaper when he walked in. She smiled up at him, but when she saw his swelled mouth and dark frown, the smile faded a little.

"Well, there you are, you good-looking thing," she greeted, dropping the paper down into her lap. "You do look better since you had a bath. But what happened to your face? Did a horse kick you?"

Despite the fact that Joe knew that she was kidding with him, he felt his face turn red at her comments.

"Yeah, it's surprising what a little soap and water can do for a person," he replied, glancing over to the corner where he had left his dirty clothes in the paper sack earlier. The sack was gone. "If you can call Bernie Graff a horse, then a horse kicked me."

The woman's dark eyes flew wide open and she stared up at him. "You mean Bernie Graff did that to you and you walked away from it in one piece?" She gaped in disbelief and a small grin pulled at the corners of her red mouth.

"Yeah," Joe replied, wanting to laugh again when she'd used the big man's first name. "I hit him with a currycomb and he put me down."

Saber's laughter filled the lobby and he grinned despite his sore mouth.

"Where are my clothes?" he asked, grinning down at her.

"If you're worrying about them," Saber said, following the direction of his gaze, "Carla Onrota will bring them back in the morning. There won't be a speck of dirt on them."

"Good," Joe said, reaching into his pocket for

some money. "How much do I owe you or her for this?"

"Nothing, it's included in the price of the room," she answered, cocking her head to one side and arching her brows slightly.

"You mean to sit there and tell me," Joe said, mock accusation in his brown eyes, "that if I didn't have any dirty clothes, I'd be paying for something I wasn't getting."

Saber looked up at him totally undaunted by his words. She blinked her eyes slowly.

"If I hadn't told you," she countered, narrowing her eyes, "you would have thought that it was a courtesy of the hotel. Although here lately," she went on, arching her brows, "Carla has almost been too busy to do the hotel guests' laundry. She almost has her hands full with just the sheets and towels."

Joe couldn't understand why that would be the case. The hotel wasn't all that big. Why would it take so much time to do perhaps twenty sheets? "Maybe she's working for someone else?" Joe ventured, a thought building in the back of his mind.

"Oh, she is," Saber replied in a snappish answer. "She's started doing laundry for Winston Haverty and his bunch of snakes. I guess that includes you now, huh?"

Saber had given words to Joe's thoughts and he expelled a deep breath. "Yeah, I guess it does."

In deep thought Joe turned and went up the stairs to his room. Unlocking the door, he crossed over to the window, opened it, sat down in a straight-backed chair, and propped his feet up on the sill.

If Carla Onrota was doing a lot of laundry for Winston Haverty's employees, that had to mean that a lot of cattle were being butchered.

Something told Joe Howard that he wouldn't have to think twice to know which pen the cattle would be taken from to be butchered for the Indians.

But he wondered, getting up and stretching out across the bed, where were the healthy cattle going?

Chapter 3

Joe Howard slept until around seven that evening. He would have slept longer but loud music from the Whispering Wind Saloon down the street jarred him wide awake with a start. He knew that there was no use in lying there on the bed and trying to go back to sleep. The only thing he would accomplish would be tossing and turning and tearing up the bed.

His stomach began rumbling and he realized that he was hungry. Getting up, he pulled on his boots, was pleased beyond words that Saber Entonelli wasn't in the lobby, and crossed the street to the café. Everyone must have been at the saloon because the café was almost empty. The food on his plate had to have been a leftover from dinner. The steak that would have been well done at dinner could have been used now to resole a pair of boots, and the fried potatoes could have been used for boot lacings. Joe remembered what the pie had been like earlier and shook his head when the same tall, redheaded waiter asked him if he wanted something sweet.

The moon was coming up over the eastern rim of the desert, and even though the wind was blowing, but then the wind was always blowing, there seemed to be a peaceful stillness all over the land.

Joe could hear a coyote, a dove, and crickets, baying, cooing, and chirping in the mountains, trees, and grass and wondered why these particular sounds were always beautiful but always sounded so lonely. He stopped and listened for a moment.

Joe was jarred from his melancholy thoughts by a burst of loud laughter from the saloon. He hadn't had a beer in a long time and the coffee hadn't been enough to quench his thirst.

Thick smoke from cigars and cigarettes and the scent of cheap perfume and cheaper whiskey reached his nose as he stepped up on the narrow plank sidewalk and could have been cut with a dull knife. Joe pushed open the squeaky batwings and shouldered his way over to the bar. There was hardly enough room for a flea at the bar that ran the length of the saloon. An upright piano was pushed up against the wall and a short, fat, bald man was running his stubby fingers idly up and down the keys. A roulette wheel was against the left wall, inviting the adventuresome to take a chance. A billiard table wasn't too far from the piano and card tables were scattered around.

The beer was a lot better than Joe imagined that it would be. It was cool and had a good bite to it. After the second sip, Joe glanced around the saloon. Every male of drinking age in Marathon must have been either at the bar or sitting at one of the tables. Joe looked up at his reflections in the frost-edged mirror and was surprised to see Winston Haverty and Bernie Graff standing at the right end of the bar.

Raw hatred still blazed in Graff's black eyes as he met Joe's gaze in the mirror. Joe hoped that he would be able to get this job finished before he had to shoot Bernie Graff. Shifting his attention away from the two men at the end of the bar, Joe looked to his left. Miles Rymer and Frank Zahn were sitting at a corner table playing poker with three other men. That left only Iggy Jennssen, Jack Lucas, and Ed Spencer missing from the seven men working for Winston Haverty.

Iggy Jennssen was no doubt sleeping at the livery and Jack Lucas was probably at the cattle pens. There was no telling where Ed Spencer was. Going on the assumption that Ed Spencer wouldn't be at the cattle pens, Joe let the thought that had been in the back of his mind for the past few hours surface. He wanted to look in Winston Haverty's desk. He was pretty sure that there would be some incriminating evidence there that would tell him all about the cattle. Maybe he would even find out who had given four McClellan saddles to Haverty, Graff, Jennssen, and Spencer. Joe was puzzled as much about the saddles as he was about the cattle.

Downing the beer, Joe faked a yawn and stretched in the small space allowed. He wanted the two men at the bar especially to think that he was sleepy and going back to the hotel.

Pushing his hat back on his head, Joe shoved his

hands down in his pockets and walked slowly out of the saloon and into the warm night air. As soon as the batwings had swung closed behind him, Joe hurried down to the livery. He wanted to be sure that Iggy Jennssen was there. If he wasn't, he was probably standing guard at the cattle pens. If he was at the livery, Joe could just tell him that he wanted to check on Serge.

As usual, the big black horse nickered low in his throat when Joe walked up to him. There was enough moonlight for Joe to see the four McClellan saddles hanging on the stalls. Easing down to the end of the livery, Joe stopped outside a closed door. He didn't have to listen too hard to hear snoring loud enough to loosen the nails in the boards coming from the other side.

Knowing that the four men were at the saloon and that Iggy Jennssen was asleep, Joe only had to account for Jack Lucas and Ed Spencer. They would probably be guarding at the cattle pens. But somehow Joe kind of doubted it. Two men couldn't possibly guard that many cows. They probably had their own watering hole.

Leaving the livery, he hurried down to the low white-washed building, went around to the back, and peeped in through the window. The bunks at the end of the room were in deep shadows. The moon didn't quite cast its light that far. Another good thing was on Joe's side. If Jack Lucas and Ed Spencer were in the building, Joe could just say that he had to see Winston Haverty.

Joe opened the door on squeaky hinges and froze

where he stood, his hand on the Colt .45. His heart beat faster as he waited for someone to come and see what had caused the noise.

But if Lucas or Spencer were inside, they were either sleeping too soundly to hear the noise, or they could have thought that it was Graff or the other men coming back. Joe didn't think that Winston Haverty would sleep in such crude accommodations. Waiting a few more seconds, Joe pushed the door farther open and stepped into the room. Giving his eyes time to adjust to the dimness, he closed the door shut behind him and waited. The silence roared in his ears and chill bumps raced up his back and arms.

When his vision finally penetrated the dimness at the end of the room, he was a little surprised and greatly relieved to see that there was no one in any of the bunks.

Turning back to his right, he hurried over to the desk, which was in front of the window. This could be a disadvantage. But he hoped that anyone seeing him at the desk would think that he was Haverty. That wouldn't work, of course, if Haverty or one of his men happened to see him there. He would just have to take the chance and hurry with the search. Hopefully, it wouldn't take too long, since there was only one long narrow drawer across the front and one deep drawer on either side.

Pulling the chair back from the desk, Joe opened the long drawer first. The only things he saw in the moon's dim light were a note pad, several envelopes, a ruler, two stubby pencils, a quill pen, and a bottle of ink.

In disappointment, he closed the drawer and opened the one on the right side of the desk. On top of a stack of papers was a dark-colored ledger. His heart began racing and his gut intuition told him that this was probably what he was looking for.

Taking the ledger, Joe squatted down, removed his hat, and eased over by the window for better light from the moon. Flipping through the pages, he really had to squint to see anything. Just as his eyes were beginning to burn and tear from the strain, he made out a name that gaped his mouth wide open. He had suspected someone from the government being on the receiving end of the better cattle instead of the Indians. But he never in his wildest imagination would have guessed that it was Senator Caleb Powers!

Joe batted his eyes several times to relieve the strain but looked quickly back at the page. He could barely make it out even though the printing was large: Shipped to Senator Caleb Powers: Two hundred and fifty head of cattle. The entry was dated two months ago. Turning the pages back, there was another entry dated two months prior to that.

Powers was the "pompous ass," as Colonel Eric McRaney had called him, who had refused to meet with Chief Keoni last year to discuss a solution to the raids on wagon trains and settlements between San Antonio and El Paso.

As Joe got to his feet and replaced the ledger in the desk, he wondered what Powers was doing with so many cattle. Was Powers buying the cattle or was he just getting them for nothing? Joe suspected the latter. Then he wondered where all the cattle were coming from in the first place. He also wondered how a man of Powers's position could take the cattle that were meant for hungry people and were a means to bring peace.

Joe was just closing the desk drawer when the front door banged open and Jack Lucas came staggering in. Joe, smelling cheap rotgut whiskey on the man all the way across the room, knew that he hadn't been in the saloon and wondered where he'd gotten it. But then he realized that it could have come from anywhere.

Joe didn't think that, in Lucas's present condition, he presented any threat, and Joe stood silent, although he did take hold of the pistol handle as he watched the man stagger down to the end bunk and crash onto it.

Giving Lucas a couple more minutes to pass out, Joe tiptoed across the room, glad he'd never gotten into the habit of wearing spurs, opened the back door, eased it shut, and left.

He'd found what he was looking for and a lot of things were falling into place, Joe thought as he walked across the street and back to the hotel. He had never met Senator Caleb Powers, but right then he would have liked to look into the eyes of a man who would refuse to meet with someone to try and resolve a bad situation then turn around and make things worse.

Was Winston Haverty selling the cattle to Powers or giving them to him? Who was selling Haverty the cattle? Was one person selling Haverty all of the cattle or did he have three suppliers? Powers was no doubt getting the healthy cattle. The Indians were getting the inferior meat. Who was getting the secondary cattle? Maybe he would learn the answer to all those questions tomorrow. Somehow this wasn't turning out to be as simple as he had thought when he left the fort.

"Are you going to stand out there all night frowning or are you going to come in here and talk to me?" Saber Entonelli's voice shocked Joe. He'd been so engrossed in his own thoughts about the cattle, Winston Haverty, and Senator Caleb Powers that he wasn't aware that he'd reached the hotel and was standing at the door. Saber was leaning against the door jamb, maybe to catch any cool breeze that might come along.

"Oh, I was just thinking about starting work tomorrow," Joe said, pushing his hat back on his head. The same irritated look flashed in her dark eyes as it had earlier when he'd mentioned having a job with Winston Haverty.

"May I tell you something?" Saber asked, narrowing her eyes and tilting her head back to look up at him. She chewed on the inside of her upper lip as she waited for his answer.

"Sure," Joe said, frowning down at her. He was puzzled at the question because she looked and sounded so serious. He would have felt better if she'd been flirting with him as she'd been earlier in the day.

"When I first saw you this morning," Saber began, folding her arms under her ample breast, "I'll admit that you did look like a first-class saddle bum and needing a bath. But after you had a bath and were

74

cleaned up, you looked like someone entirely different. You seem to be masquerading as something you're not. I'm a pretty good judge of character, Mr. Howard, and I know that you don't need to be working for Winston Haverty. You have an ulterior motive for being here." Shrewdness and certainty were in her voice and eyes.

Joe Howard knew that he was staring down at the black-haired woman who had a solemn expression on her face. He was amazed at her astuteness. Most women in her position just rented out rooms, took the money, and the next day couldn't tell one hotel guest from a stranger in the street.

"You could be right," Joe said, arching his brows and grinning down at her. "Why don't you like Winston Haverty?" he asked. "He seemed all right to me. Just a little short."

For a second the wild notion that Haverty might have insulted her or turned down her advances popped into Joe's mind. Maybe she wanted some kind of revenge. Maybe if she could turn Joe against working for Haverty, that would mean one less employee and his business would suffer from it. Joe remembered the old adage about a woman scorned. But the way she pressed her mouth into a thin line told him that it was something entirely different. Saber just didn't like the man.

"Would you like some coffee?" she suddenly asked, a slight smile easing across her face. "You'll be safe," she went on when he frowned down at her again. "I promise not to lay a hand on you. Unless you want me to."

"Oh, I didn't mean that," Joe said quickly, feeling

75

his face turn red again. "Some coffee sounds good. I hope it's better than that stuff at the café."

"Everything I have here is better than you'll get anywhere else," she said over her shoulder as Joe followed her into the hotel and to a side room which apparently served as her living quarters. A table, two chairs, and a stove were at one end of the room. A dresser, a sofa, and apparently a bed behind a drawn curtain were at the other end.

Joe was at a loss for words as he sat down at the table. It didn't take long for her to have a fire going in the small black iron stove and soon coffee was bubbling away in the black shiny pot. Joe thought that he'd died and gone to heaven when she sliced off a good-sized piece of yellow pound cake and set it before him.

"You ask why I don't like Winston Haverty," she began, sitting down at the table across from him and taking a sip of coffee. "You probably aren't aware of this but all of the cattle in those pens should be going to an Indian chief and his people who live at a camp in Elephant Mountain."

If Saber had told Joe Howard that his hair was on fire, it wouldn't have taken him any more by surprise than what she'd just said. Not that it really mattered one way or the other but Joe had thought that it would be some sort of secret about the cattle.

Joe, still sure that it was best that no one know who he was, decided to keep on playing the part of a man just needing a job. Maybe in his case, ignorance could educate.

"Well, I think that's a good idea," Joe said,

chewing on a piece of the best cake he'd tasted in a long time. He could feel the hairs stand up on the back of his neck and was sure that she could see them also. "From what I can understand, the Indians don't have enough food to eat and that's one reason for all of the unrest out here. If my family was hungry," he went on, after washing down the cake with a sip of coffee that was strong enough to grown hair on a man's elbow, "I'd do everything I could to feed them. The Indians are no different. They feel things, the same as you and I."

Noticing the aggravated look on Saber's face, Joe hushed and took another bite of cake.

"Apparently you didn't hear me say that all of the cows were *supposed* to be going to the Indians," she informed him in a flat voice. Her eyes snapped and she pressed her mouth into a thin line.

"Well, if all of the cows are supposed to be going to the Indians," Joe began, washing the cake down with another sip of coffee, "why aren't they? How do you know that they're not?" He arched his brows skeptically.

Saber leaned back in the chair, expelled a disgruntled breath, and shook her head slowly. She pulled her red mouth snidely to one side.

"I know"—she drew the word out and narrowed her eyes—"because the previous owner of those cows spent the night here at the hotel two weeks ago. As long as Silas Bruell was in town, all of the cows were kept in one large pen east of town. But the minute he left, that low-down rat Winston Haverty divided the cows into those three groups. You can probably guess what the three groups are and who's getting the tail end of the bunch."

Joe Howard felt as if Saber Entonelli had reached inside his head and had pulled out all his thoughts, suspicions, and accusations. He must have been staring at her again with his mouth wide open because she started laughing at him.

"What's the matter, Mr. Howard?" she asked shrewdly, giving him a sideways look. Then pursing her lips, she turned her head and looked at him straight on. "Why are you speechless all of a sudden? Are you surprised that some women have a little more between their ears than just gray matter? Are you surprised that I'm more than just a pretty face?"

"Did Silas Bruell tell you that the Indians were supposed to get all of the cows?" Joe asked, flabbergasted again at what she'd said. She nodded, drawing her mouth into a thin mocking smile and batting her eyes slowly. "Would you happen to know who is getting the other cows?"

Since Joe already knew that Senator Caleb Powers was getting some of the cattle and those would probably be the ones in the first pen, he wondered if she knew about Powers and who was getting the other grade of beef.

If she knew all of that, it meant that someone working for Winston Haverty had to have a big mouth. Joe couldn't see her getting cozy enough with Bernie Graff for it to be him. But then he couldn't see that happening with any of the other men either. Except maybe Jack Lucas. He wasn't too bad-looking, with sandy-colored hair and light blue eyes.

He weighed about ten pounds more than Joe and was a few inches shorter.

"I would just happen to know that Senator Caleb Powers gets the best cattle," she said slowly, "and that the other good cattle go to someone in Marfa." A smugness crept across her olive face and danced in her dark eyes. Joe could tell that she was enjoying this.

Joe dropped his hand on the table and sat there in a state of absolute shock. He wondered how she knew about all this, and he would probably ask her about it before he left.

Suddenly the image of a well-dressed senator giving McClellan saddles to Winston Haverty and the other three men took shape in Joe's mind. A senator would have access to forts and could probably take anything he wanted, including McClellan saddles. Joe wondered if any money had been exchanged. Maybe not. McClellan saddles were popular with the army but not that expensive. Two cows, three at the most, would probably pay for one saddle.

Joe knew that Marfa wasn't too far from Elephant Mountain. If anyone began asking questions about meat shipments in that area, it could be said that they were going to the Indians and then be diverted to someone over in Marfa.

Everything fell into place now and Joe wondered why Colonel Eric McRaney hadn't thought about the diversion or why Chief Keoni or at least some of his braves hadn't seen what was going on and done something about it.

"Now may I ask you a question?" Joe asked, drawing his brows into a slight frown. "Just how did you know or learn about all of this?"

Saber looked at Joe for a second before she threw back her head and began laughing.

"You have your secrets," she said, swallowing and taking a deep breath, "and I have mine."

Joe thought that he'd let her enjoy the moment for a while. "Well, it could only have been Jack Lucas who would get drunk enough to shoot off his mouth and tell someone something that he shouldn't." He felt bad when the triumphant smile began slowly leaving her face.

"How did you figure out that it was Jack?" she asked before thinking. She turned red when she saw a grin spreading across his face.

"I didn't know until just then," Joe answered, shaking his head. "It was just a lucky guess." He drained his coffee cup and stood up. "Well, I guess I'd better turn in. It's going to be a long day tomorrow."

"If you're half as smart as you think you are," Saber said, giving Joe a scathing look, her dark eyes blazing in contempt, "you'll be able to get all of this straightened out in just a little while."

Joe really felt bad now about hurting her feelings but he didn't want her getting the idea that he was just a saddle bum riding through who couldn't figure things out for himself.

Nevertheless he was a little ashamed of himself for taking away some of her pride and self-esteem. Saber Entonelli probably had a respectable standing in

Marathon and would be living here long after he had left.

"Look," he said, walking around to her side of the table and smiling down at her, "a lucky guess had nothing to do with me knowing that Jack Lucas was the one who told you about Winston Haverty and Caleb Powers. I was in the office"—he made a gesture with his thumb over his shoulder toward the building across the street—"when Lucas came staggering in. Can you keep a secret?"

Joe knew that he was taking a great chance in revealing his true identity and a knot of caution pulled in his stomach. But maybe, and the possibility of that happening was way in the back of his mind, she could help him.

"Of course," she assured him, the insulted expression leaving her face to be replaced with an expectant and excited smile.

"I am not the saddle bum that everyone seemed to think I was when I first rode into town." He wanted to burst out laughing at the intent look in her dark eyes. "I am an army scout from Fort Davis. I'm here to find out why Chief Keoni and his people aren't getting the meat that our benevolent government promised them."

Joe couldn't stop sarcasm from creeping into his voice. He certainly wasnt prepared for what happened next.

"Oh, that makes me so happy," Saber squealed, a wide smile racing across her face. Before Joe knew what was happening to him, she jumped up from the chair, threw her arms around his neck, and planted a

81

resounding kiss right on his mouth. Embarrassed, she stepped back, a red hue on her face, and her black eyes were wide in shock.

Joe Howard hadn't met many women in the past few months who he'd wanted to kiss but he had second thoughts about Saber Entonelli. Without giving much thought to what he was doing, Joe reached out, wrapped his arms around her ample body, drew her against him, and kissed her in a soft, gentle way they both enjoyed.

"That wasn't bad," he said, raising his head and grinning down at her.

"No, it wasn't," she answered, taking a deep breath and dropping her hands from his shoulders.

"Well," he said, taking a step backward. "It is getting late and I do have to be up early in the morning." He walked to the door but turned around and looked at her. Saber had sat back down at the table, a red glow still on her face. "Please, don't tell anyone who I am."

"I won't," she promised in a low voice. "I'm just glad that you're here to help those people. I hope you see to it that Winston Haverty gets what he deserves."

"I'll do just that," Joe said, nodding deeply and winking at her.

Joe went upstairs, undressed, and sprawled out on the bed. He hoped that he hadn't done the wrong thing in telling Saber Entonelli who he really was. But something told him that she was probably one of the few people in Marathon he could trust.

As Joe lay there on the bed in the darkness, he wondered if Winston Haverty had meant for it to be kept a secret what was being done with the cattle. There was no doubt in Joe's mind at all that Senator Caleb Powers would want his part in the deal kept a secret. If his constituents knew that he was involved in a dirty deal against the Indians, and if he was counterproductive in a way to stop the raids, it could have a bearing on his next reelection.

Suddenly Joe was hit with a question that he hadn't thought of before. Where were all these cattle coming from? He knew that they just didn't fly into Marathon. Where was Silas Bruell getting the cattle?

Joe took a deep, irritated breath, put his arms under his head, and stared up toward the ceiling. A cool breeze was coming in through the opened window but it was still hot in the room. It seemed that the more answers he got to his questions, the more questions he got to be answered. Maybe Saber would know something more about the cattle in the morning. He would ask her then. Knowing that he couldn't accomplish anymore tonight, Joe turned over on his side and went to sleep.

He had hoped that his sleep and dreams would be pleasant. But for some reason, that hope didn't come true. Even though the window was open and a lot of time had passed, the cool breeze blowing didn't take out enough heat to make any difference. Maybe that contributed to his bad dreams.

He and Chief Keoni were standing on a high bluff overlooking a river where a lot of fat cattle were grazing on tall, lush green grass. At first the clear water ran smoothly over the pebbles and the fat cows moseyed along. A dozen children were skipping rocks across the water and laughing. Suddenly a cracking sound broke the stillness. Joe looked across the river to an even higher bluff and couldn't believe what he saw.

Bernie Graff's huge body seemed to fill the entire sky. A strong wind began blowing, whipping at his long black hair and beard. The cracking sound came from a long black bullwhip he held in his right hand and waved over his head. The whip cracked again and Joe heard the children scream. Tearing his gaze from Graff, Joe looked back down at the river.

The cattle were still grazing but all of the fat had disappeared from their bodies and he could count every rib. Instead of the grass being plentiful and green, it was now sparse, dry, and brown. Joe was horrified when he saw why the children had screamed. The once clear, smooth-running water had turned to deep red blood and was bubbling up close to the bank.

Joe seemed to be moving in slow motion as he turned his head to look at Chief Keoni. Keoni was taking an arrow from the quiver on his back and putting it to the bow in his skeletal hand that up until a few seconds ago had looked firm and healthy. But before Keoni could send the arrow flying, the laughter of a mad man filled the air along with another cracking sound as Graff snapped the whip in the air and jerked the bow and arrow from Keoni's hands.

The Indian began withering right before Joe's disbelieving eyes and the last word he was able to mutter before he crumpled to the ground at Joe's feet was "food."

Joe had always been able to awaken at a certain time. It was as if he had a clock set inside his head. A thin slit of orange was dividing the earth from the sky when he awoke the next morning. He was on his back when his eyes finally opened. His mouth was open and dry and his hands were hanging over the side of the narrow bed. His fingers were tingling and it seemed to take forever to stand up and get his shirt on and buttoned.

Joe knew that Winston Haverty had told him to come to work at sunup. But he didn't want Haverty to get the impression that he'd jump when Haverty snapped his fingers.

Joe was in a hurry to get to the cattle pens but took enough time to go by the café for a cup of coffee and a biscuit and a fried egg. The sun was a red ball and had already cleared the horizon as he left the café and walked nonchalantly into the building.

Winston Haverty was sitting behind the desk, anger written all over his small tanned face. His green-flecked brown eyes were snapping when he looked up as Joe came through the door. Joe wondered if he was mad because he was late. Haverty's butter-colored hair was neatly combed, and even though he was dressed in tan pants and light blue shirt, he still looked small.

"Well, it's about time you showed up," Graff said sarcastically, glaring at Joe. He reached up and touched his right cheek where Joe had hit him with the currycomb yesterday. He was sitting on a straight chair against the wall. The chair was almost lost beneath him and Joe had to struggle to keep from smiling. Graff looked as if he were suspended in midair.

"Mr. Haverty told me to be here at sunup," Joe snapped in response, pulling his chin down. He glanced out the window. "The sun is up. I am here." He shrugged his shoulders.

Miles Rymer and Frank Zahn hadn't been in the livery yesterday when Joe and Graff had had their verbal and physical altercation. Up until now they'd never known of anyone going up against the big man. Their eyes were wide in surprise. Winston Haverty jarred everyone into silence when he slammed his fist down on the desk.

"I'm not going to tell you two again," he yelled, his beady brown eyes flashing in aggravated anger. "If this keeps up, I'm going to shoot both of you myself. I don't have time for this!"

Joe wanted to laugh as he eased over by Miles Rymer and Frank Zahn. But from the furious scowl on Haverty's tanned face, he knew that it was no laughing matter. "What's the matter with him?" Joe asked Rymer in a low voice.

"Somebody went through Mr. Haverty's desk last night," Rymer answered in the same tone of voice but, nevertheless, Haverty heard the question and answer. Even though the room was already getting warm, shivers went up and down Joe's back while sweat dampened under his arm pits.

"Why would anyone want to go through your desk?" Joe asked, shifting his weight from his right foot over to the other and hooking his thumbs over his belt. Only on the outside did he appear calm and curious. But on the inside he was a nervous wreck. He wondered if someone had seen him going in or coming out of Haverty's office last night. Was Jack Lucas only pretending to be drunk? Had he seen Joe and told Winston Haverty that someone had been in his office? Joe also wondered if there was anything else incriminating against Senator Caleb Powers other than what he'd seen in the folder.

"There are things in my desk," Haverty raged through clenched teeth as he braced both hands on the desk and stood up, "that are private."

"Is anything missing?" Joe asked, almost holding his breath. He knew that he hadn't taken anything, but apparently Haverty had a special way of placing things in the desk and Joe, in the darkness, hadn't replaced the ledger in the right way.

"No, nothing is missing," Haverty shouted, pressing his lips tightly together and lowering himself slowly back down in the chair, "but it's no one's business what is in my books and desk."

All of the men were staring at Winston Haverty. The room was quiet for a few seconds until a low moan sounded from the far end of the room. Jack Lucas was finally coming around. Joe turned around and watched him struggle to his feet and come stumbling toward them.

"What in the devil is all of the noise and yelling about?" Lucas mumbled with a thick tongue. He dug at his bloodshot eyes with the heels of his hand. Turning his head slowly, as if it took all of his effort, he scowled at each man in the room.

"Well, have you finally decided to join the land of the living and sober?" Haverty asked coldly, a snarl on his mouth. "Jack, were you here all night? Did you see anyone come in?"

Joe's heart skipped a beat, his breath didn't reach all the way to his lungs, and he could feel sweat begin rolling down his back as he watched Winston Haverty and waited for Jack Lucas to answer the question.

"Mr. Haverty," Lucas said in a slurred voice, while licking his dry mouth with a thick tongue, "a herd of buffalo could have come through here last night and I wouldn't have heard them. Why do you want to know if somebody was in here for? Is something missing?"

"No, nothing is missing," Haverty said, expelling a disgruntled breath as he shot Lucas a repulsive look. "But someone went through my desk last night. Everything is messed around."

"What would be in your desk that anybody would want to see?" Graff asked, a blank expression in his black eyes. Apparently, Joe surmised, Graff wasn't as much in Haverty's confidence as Joe had thought he would be. Joe had thought that Graff was Haverty's right-hand man and would have told him everything.

"Don't ask stupid questions, Graff," Haverty snapped, glaring over at the big man. He took the disarranged papers and folder from the drawer, banged them against the top of the desk, got them all straight, and replaced them, slamming the drawer shut.

Joe watched Winston Haverty take a long breath,

swallow hard, and stand up again. Joe was still amazed at the little man's size.

"Well," Haverty said resolutely, making a smacking sound with his mouth pulled in against his teeth, "there's a lot of work to do so we might as well get to it. Graff," he went on, looking up at the big man, who had stood up, "I want you and Howard, no that won't do," he said, shaking his head quickly, "you'd probably end up killing each other." He stopped and chewed thoughtfully on the inside of his mouth. "Graff," he began again, "I want you and Rymer to cut out about a hundred head of cows for Powers, then use the Mexicans who went to Marfa last month to help you drive them. Powers can come and get them at the holding pen close to town. There's no need for you to drive them to his place."

Graff threw Joe a cunning look as he and Rymer walked out the door.

While Joe waited for his assignment, he wondered if all these men already had crews in mind to help them with their duties. Haverty took a white piece of paper from the drawer in front of him, made a notation on it, then looked up at Joe.

"Howard, do you know where Brewster is?" he asked, irritation still evident in his being late although there was still no surprise or accusation in the frowning look he gave Joe as he waited for his answer.

"Yeah," Joe said, nodding, knowing instantly that he and one of the other men were going to take the cattle from the middle pen to someone there. "It's just a little northwest of here."

"I know where it is," Haverty snapped, his eyes blazing. "I just wanted to know if you did. I want you and Jack Lucas to use the same men who went with Graff and Lucas to Marfa last month, to take a hundred cows out of the second pen and drive them to a holding pen just north of town."

There was no doubt now in Joe's mind who would be getting the rest of the cattle. Poor Keoni, Joe thought sadly. He and his people needed the meat a lot worse than Powers and whoever was at Marfa.

Iggy Jennssen and Frank Zahn would be the ones left to take the cattle to the Indians after they were slaughtered.

"Where is Ed Spencer?" Joe asked, looking around the room for the extra man.

"Not that it's any of your business," Haverty answered, frowning at Joe, "but he had to go to San Angelo to see about another shipment of cows."

"Will someone be in Brewster to sign for the cattle?" Joe asked, walking toward the door. Jack Lucas was stumbling along behind him.

"Don't worry about it," Haverty called out. "Lucas will know what to do when you get there."

As Joe opened the door, he glanced back at Iggy Jennssen. It suddenly dawned on him how relaxed the man with the odd-colored hair was. When Joe had first come into the room, Jennssen seemed to be as jittery as a bridegroom. Was he afraid that Joe would be sent with him to take the cows to Keoni? Had he been afraid that Joe would see what the Indians really ended up getting? Joe didn't know how far the cattle had been driven before reaching Mara-

90

thon but he knew for certain that they would never reach Elephant Mountain on the hoof. Joe wondered why that would matter to Iggy Jennssen.

Joe wanted to laugh when they stepped out into the bright sunlight and Jack Lucas slapped his hands over his eyes and moaned as if he were in deep pain.

"I'm going to quit drinking someday," Lucas said, rubbing his face briskly with both hands. "I swear I am." He shook his head and slowly eased his eyes up to meet Joe's. "It tastes sooooo good at the moment. But this"—he made a face and wagged his tongue—"just isn't worth it." Lucas shivered and swallowed hard then made another bad face.

This time Joe did laugh. There had been one or two times when he knew exactly how Lucas was feeling. Reaching out, he slapped the miserable-looking man on the shoulders.

"Maybe some coffee will help," Joe suggested. He would have mentioned food but he didn't want to see Lucas lose what he had in his stomach right there in the middle of the street.

"No, we don't have time for that," Lucas replied, shaking his head doggedly. "Mr. Haverty always wants things done in a hurry."

Joe knew from past experience that Lucas needed something in his stomach and a few extra minutes wouldn't make that much difference. But he didn't want to press his luck too far, and remembering that Saber already knew Jack Lucas, Joe took hold of his arm and pulled him toward the hotel.

Opening the hotel door, Joe smelled the coffee and knew that Saber was up. She opened the door to her living quarters when Joe knocked, and a wide smile raced across her face when she saw him but quickly disappeared when she saw Jack Lucas standing behind him.

"Which cattle are you taking to whom?" she asked acidly, arching her brows, a knowing look in her dark eyes. Without being told, she took two cups from pegs on the wall, filled them with her strong black brew, and handed them to Joe and Lucas. Joe watched Lucas and shook his head in mute sympathy. The man had to use both hands to get the cup up to his mouth.

"Jack and I are going to have the pleasure of taking a hundred head of cattle to a place in Brewster," Joe replied contritely, switching his attention from Lucas, who was almost gulping the strong coffee, back to Saber.

She looked especially pretty this morning in a deep lavender dress, with a square neck edged in pink lace. It set off her black hair, dark eyes, and olive skin. Her hair was wound around her head in a long braid, with curls in the center, giving her a regal look. He must have been staring at her because a pink hue began creeping up her neck above the tops of her bared breasts. He let his eyes linger on her mouth, remembering the two kisses last night. He wondered why he hadn't dreamed about that.

"Is there something missing?" she asked, batting her eyes uncomfortably, folding her hands in front of her.

"Oh, no," Joe answered, flashing a smile at her. "Everything is right where it belongs. I was just thinking."

"About what?" she asked, taking a step toward him, a different kind of look coming into her eyes. Catching herself, she stopped abruptly and took a deep breath.

"About how long it's going to take Jack and me to drive a hundred head of cattle to Brewster," Joe answered, picking up the coffee cup to give his hands something to do. For some reason, they were shaking.

"You and Jack are going to Brewster?" she repeated, switching her gaze over to Lucas and frowning at him. "I thought you were supposed to—"

"Not now," Joe interrupted, knowing that she was about to forget her promise and, in her surprise, blurt out who he was. But glancing down at Jack Lucas guzzling another cup of coffee, he knew that Lucas wouldn't have caught on if one of them had drawn him a picture.

Joe drained his cup, put it down on the table, and tapped Lucas on the shoulder. Lucas stood up and surprised both Joe and Saber by quickly leaning over and kissing her on the cheek.

"What was all that about?" Joe asked when they were outside, a funny feeling around his heart, in the middle of his stomach, and in his knees.

"What?" Lucas asked, giving Joe a sideways glance, looking more sober than any drunk Joe had ever seen. Joe knew that the coffee couldn't have worked that fast. "Oh, you mean that kiss? If you're having any second thoughts about Saber, don't worry about it. She and I are only friends."

"I guess we'd better get some men together," Joe

suggested, feeling silly as he walked in long strides toward the livery. He knew that Iggy Jennssen would probably already be gone from there along with Frank Zahn.

"Yeah, you're right," Lucas answered, a stillness suddenly coming over his face as he took the regular saddle from the stall and slung a blanket over a buckskin's back. "By the way, the next time you go through Winston Haverty's desk, be sure to put everything back the way you found it."

Joe Howard's heart literally stopped in his chest as he stared at Jack Lucas. He had slung the blanket and saddle on Serge but his hands froze on the saddle horn and the cantle.

Chapter 4

Joe Howard felt as if someone had dropped a sledge-hammer on his head. Lucas had known that Joe had looked in Winston Haverty's desk last night! Why had he lied to Haverty about not hearing Joe in the building? Lucas certainly had no reason for being afraid of Joe. For all intents and purposes, Joe Howard was just another saddle bum passing through Marathon who just happened to be at the right place at the right time to land a job. Jack Lucas was already working for Winston Haverty. It seemed to Joe that if Lucas could turn the tables on an intruder, that would put him one up in Haverty's eyes.

Joe remembered something else that was strange about Jack Lucas. Why had he shared his information so freely with Saber Entonelli? Why had he carried on his drunk act when they were having coffee at her place and then sobered up as soon as they got outside?

Joe was positive that no one could sober up that fast. He had really smelled the cheap whiskey on the man last night but that didn't actually mean that Lucas had been drinking.

Joe knew that he couldn't get any of these questions answered by just standing their gaping at the smirking man standing before him. "What kind of game are you playing, Lucas?" Joe asked, throwing the cinch over Serge. He turned around to face Lucas. "You were certainly a convincing drunk. But I don't think the coffee at Saber Entonelli's sobered you up that fast."

It seemed to take forever for Lucas to take a long breath, expel it, and even start to answer Joe's question.

"I guess it could be said that we both are playing some kind of game," Lucas said finally, pulling the cinch tighter on the saddle. "I am no more of a drunk than you are a saddle bum just passing through."

Joe was as surprised at Lucas's astuteness as he'd been at Saber's. If Lucas and Saber had seen through him so easily, why hadn't Winston Haverty? Maybe Haverty's mind had been too preoccupied with other matters. Like the cattle for Powers and how to cheat.

"How long have you worked for Haverty?" Joe asked, tightening the cinch and swinging up on Serge before revealing too much about himself.

"About three months," Lucas answered, swinging the horse around. "I don't know if I should tell you this," Lucas went on, pulling his mouth to one side, "but I think we both have a secret identity and I believe that we're both here for the same reason."

Joe watched as Jack Lucas pulled in a long breath, arched his brows, and then as if throwing caution to the wind, shrugged his shoulders and said, "I'm an undercover Texas Ranger. There have been a lot of cattle rustled around Waco and San Angelo and are supposed to be out here in this area. Some of them are probably in the first and second pens at Haverty's."

Joe Howard didn't know how many more surprises he could handle today. But if he kept on getting any more, his head would probably explode. In the first place, he couldn't believe that Jack Lucas was a Texas Ranger. He just didn't fit Joe's idea of what a ranger would look like. For one thing, Lucas was too short. Joe stood five feet seven and Lucas had to look up at him about an inch. Joe thought he had about ten pounds too much on him. But he grinned when he thought about David and Goliath.

"There you go, grinning again," Lucas said, frowning slightly and riding a little ahead of Joe toward the east end of town. "Didn't Graff teach you a lesson about grinning yesterday?"

"I was just thinking about you and a giant," Joe replied, touching his sore mouth and pulling his hat down lower over his eyes against the sun's bright rays. "I guess I'd better tell you that I'm a scout from Fort Davis. I've been sent here to find out why Chief Keoni and his people aren't getting good meat the way they're supposed to from the government."

Lucas jerked around in the saddle and stared at Joe. He looked as surprised as Joe had felt a few minutes ago when he'd learned who Lucas was.

"Have you been using the drunk act since you've

been working for Haverty?'' Joe asked. He knew that if Winston Haverty found out that Lucas was a Ranger, he stood a better chance of getting killed than Joe did.

"Yeah, a couple of times," Lucas said, nodding slowly and pulling his mouth into a tight line against his teeth. "This has turned into a bigger operation than we expected it to be. We thought it could be cleared up in only a few weeks. But it seems to be dragging on. I've usually worked with Graff in driving cattle to Brewster."

"If Senator Caleb Powers is getting the best cattle," Joe said as they approached an adobe hut where five Mexican men were sitting in the shade, "and the Indians are getting the worst, who is getting the ones that we're driving to Brewster? Since you already know that Powers is getting cattle meant for the Indians, why haven't you arrested him?"

"Now, that's good questions," Lucas said, a tolerant smile on his face, as he and Joe dismounted, "and even after three months, I hate to say that I don't know."

Apparently all five of the Mexican men knew Lucas because they stood up and smiled as he approached. Joe was dismayed when Lucas spoke to them in English. He'd guessed that Lucas would use Spanish. Joe was even further dismayed when the older of the five answered in English. But the accent was so deep that it could have been cut with a knife. Joe listened as Lucas told the men that Joe was going to Brewster instead of Graff. A deep sullen frown pulled the stocky, dark-skinned man's bushy black brows together. He shifted his intense black eyes from Lucas over to Joe before looking around at the other four men.

"I do not understand the cause for change," the Mexican said, looking back at Lucas. "Why aren't we going with you and Graff to Brewster? That is how it has been in the past few months."

Joe decided that if he didn't step in and say something, this man would give Lucas a hard time.

"Mr. Haverty thought that it would be a good idea if everybody changed up," Joe said in a flat voice. The Mexican stiffened and moved his eyes slowly from Lucas over to Joe. The army scout felt as if he'd been hit with a bucket of black ice. He wanted to reach for the security of the Colt .45 buckled around his waist but knew that would just be asking for trouble. Something told him that the man glaring at him would know how to use the Joslyn pistol strapped around his pudgy middle. Joe would wonder later where he had gotten it.

"Señor, my name is Armando Cavazos," the Mexican informed him arrogantly, giving Joe a level, threatening look. "I do not know you and I am not taking any orders from you."

"Mr. Cavazos, I don't care if your name is Porfirio Diaz," Joe shot back, a cold tone in his voice and eyes. This time he did rest his hand on the handle of the pistol. "Winston Haverty told Mr. Lucas and me to come and get you to help us drive some cattle to Brewster. You don't want to make Mr. Haverty angry, now do you?"

It must have been the mention of Winston

Haverty's anger—and Cavazos must have seen it at one time or another and didn't want to experience it again—that caused him to take a deep, relenting breath.

"All right," he said, shoving his hands down into the tops of his pockets. "We will do it your way." Then he hurriedly added. "This time."

Of the five men, Cavazos must have had the best command of English, because he turned to the others and explained in Spanish what had just transpired. Joe wasn't disappointed when the four men looked past Cavazos and at him with the same hostile glare in their eyes. One tall, extremely thin man took a step forward and Cavazos stopped him.

"Is there going to be any trouble with him?" Joe asked, a knot forming in his stomach. He loosened the Colt .45 in the holster.

This job was becoming a lot harder than he'd imagined. It had been his plan to ride into Marathon, find the cattle, have the sheriff arrest whoever had them, hire some men, and drive the cattle to Chief Keoni at Elephant Mountain. The theory had been simple. Implementing that theory was what was turning out to be so difficult.

But so far the only part of his plan that had worked out was that he had found the cattle in Marathon. If Colonel Eric McRaney had even intimated that there would be three groups of cattle, that Senator Caleb Powers was involved in all this, and that he would come up against two men like Bernie Graff and Armando Cavazos, he would have said no thanks and gone fishing. Now he was exerting authority over a

Texas Ranger.

"No, señor," Cavazos replied almost meekly, turning back around to face Joe and Jack Lucas. There was a sinister grin on his broad face with its wide, jaw-length sideburns. Joe knew that another obstacle had just been added to the already long list of things that he would have to watch. Cavazos was more cunning than Graff, and Joe realized that he'd have to keep a close watch on him.

"Well," Jack Lucas said, "let's all mount up and get going. Hanging around here won't get things done. We still have to get our grub sacks together." He'd stood silent the entire time that Joe and Cavazos had been arguing back and forth. Joe had watched from the corner of his eye and noticed that the Ranger had kept his hand close to his Remington.

Joe swung up and turned Serge back toward town and the cattle pens. Jack Lucas rode up beside him, a contemplative expression on his narrow face. "Do you know how close Armando Cavazos was to drawing down on you?" He spaced the words out slowly. "That man wanted to kill you just then!"

Joe looked at Lucas and expelled the breath that he just realized he'd been holding.

"Yeah, I know," Joe answered, pulling in a lung full of air. "I was hoping that you had your hand on that Remington." He expelled the breath and smiled nervously at Lucas. Joe had had his life threatened countless times but each time was no less scary than the first time.

Joe Howard was no stranger to having guns drawn on him. But usually there had been time for at least a short argument before bullets began flying. He had laid eyes on this big Mexican only a few minutes ago and already the man wanted to kill him.

God, he wished that he were fishing!

Before they went to the cattle pens, Lucas led the way to the café, went inside, and soon returned with a grub sack. "Courtesy of Winston Haverty," Lucas said to the frowning question in Joe's eyes.

"Well, with that and what I've got," Joe said, "we shouldn't get too hungry."

Joe, Lucas, and the five Mexicans reached the cattle pens and Joe was surprised and angered that only a few of the cattle in the third pen were missing. He had thought that all the cows would be gone, as were those in the first pen. Graff, Rymer, and his men had already emptied the pen with the cattle meant for Senator Caleb Powers. There were still over a hundred sickly-looking cows left behind in the third pen. Joe and Lucas exchanged knowing looks.

"Well, let's cut out the hundred head and get started toward Brewster," Joe said contritely, riding up to the gate and sliding back the long pole.

Joe, Lucas, and two of the Mexicans rode into the pen, leaving Cavazos and the other two men outside. It didn't take long, but longer than Joe would have liked, to cut out the hundred head and start northwest out of Marathon to Brewster. Too bad these cattle couldn't be going to the Indians.

"Haverty never did answer my question this morning," Joe said as he rode through the gate and waited for Lucas to close it and put the pole across it.

"What did you want to know?" Lucas asked,

swinging up on the horse.

"I asked him if there would be anyone in Brewster to sign a ticket for these cattle," Joe answered. Maybe that someone would be able to tell Joe why the Indians were getting such bad meat when no one else seemed to know. "How did you work it last time?"

"All we did last month," Lucas said, wiping a blue bandanna across his wet face, "was drive them to a holding pen that Haverty mentioned. Then we left." The sun was out in all its fury. Sweat rolled down Joe's back and white salt stains circled under his arm.

"Wasn't anybody there?" Joe persisted, narrowing his eyes as he removed his hat and pushed his wet hair back out of his face. That made no sense at all. No one would go off and leave that many good cows without a guard.

"Only a kid who was throwing some hay out," Lucas answered, taking a swig of water from the canteen.

"Do you have any idea who's getting these cattle?" Joe asked, an uneasy feeling pulling a knot in the pit of his stomach.

"No," Lucas answered, shaking his head slowly. "That's the odd thing about it. It's no secret that Senator Caleb Powers is getting his share of the cattle. The Indians are getting—"

"We all know what the Indians are getting," Joe interrupted, gritting his teeth so hard that a knot stood out in his jaw.

The seven men had been riding a half-circle behind and to the sides of the cattle and were about a quarter of a mile from Marathon when their thoughts were interrupted by the sounds of rifle shots. For an instant Joe froze in the saddle and his heart almost refused to go on beating. Jerking the Colt .45 from the holster, Joe looked all around him. But the only threatening thing he could see was the hate-filled gleam in Armando Cavazos's black eyes.

"What the devil was that?" Joe asked, tightening his hold on the reins. The rifle shot had spooked Serge and he wanted to rear up.

"It would be my guess," Lucas said almost calmly, as though he had more or less been expecting the shots, "that Iggy Jennssen and Frank Zahn and the men are about to start dressing out the cows for the Indians."

Joe had looked away from Lucas for an instant but, at his remark, jerked back around so fast that he heard his neck bone pop. "What do you mean, 'dressing out the cows for the Indians'?" Joe asked, staring at the Ranger. He'd thought all along that the cows were driven to Chief Half Moon at Elephant Mountain. "Doesn't Keoni get his meat on the hoof?" Joe didn't want to believe what he already knew.

Before Lucas could answer, Armando Cavazos threw back his head and boisterous laughter burst from his lungs.

"It would seem that you are not as smart as you thought, gringo." All of Cavazos's animosity toward Joe was in the word. Joe wondered if the big Mexican had been this hard to get along with on the last trip.

"What is he talking about?" Joe asked, looking at Jack Lucas. He didn't want to believe what he was thinking and what he was sure Lucas was going to tell him.

"The cows that the Indians get are slaughtered and dressed out before the Indians get the meat," Lucas said, dropping his head then looking at Joe sideways.

"You're joking," Joe said cynically, drawing his brows together in a tight frown. When Lucas shook his head in answer, Joe looked off in the direction of the shots. Things were beginning to make a little more sense to him now. Joe knew that the Indians would use every possible piece of a cow that they could. He was sure that they would even use the miserable-looking hides if they could get them. Keoni had told them as much the other night.

"How is that meat taken to Keoni?" Joe asked, turning slowly back to Lucas. McRaney had already told him but he wanted to see if the stories would be the same.

"It's dressed out, salted down, put in gunny sacks, and then hauled in a wagon to him," Lucas answered, holding Joe's gaze intently.

Joe was pretty sure that Jack Lucas knew what he was thinking. The Indians were getting the short end of the stick again. Give them just enough to satisfy them until the next shipment, along with some lame excuse, and maybe they wouldn't go on any kind of raid.

Joe knew that he should have insisted on going on the drive to the Indian camp at Elephant Mountain with Iggy Jennssen. After all, he had come to Marathon to find out what was happening to the meat for the Indians. But that would probably have made Winston Haverty suspicious of him. An idea was forming in Joe's mind and suddenly a surge of excitement washed over him.

The drive from Marathon to Brewster was long, hot, and tedious. The first night out was tense. The mountainous terrain didn't offer much water and they counted themselves lucky when they found a small, slow-running stream. The cattle weren't hard to control after they had water and were grazing on the meager grass.

Joe and Lucas got their grub sacks, made flat bread and coffee, then sliced off several thick pieces of salt pork and fried it. Cavazos and his men had tortillas, refried beans, and pulque. Joe had tried the milky brew once but it was a little too much for his stomach. He shivered when he thought about the potent stuff. A man would really have to hate his stomach to put that stuff in it on a regular basis.

"Cavazos, why don't you take the first watch," Joe said, kicking out his bedroll and dropping down on it. "Lucas can take the second, and I'll take the last." Joe could see and feel the belligerence building up in the big Mexican. Graff probably hadn't had any trouble out of the man because they were probably all in on the same kind of deal and weren't worried about anything happening to them. They probably hadn't even bothered to post a guard.

But Joe had something else in mind. Joe was pretty sure that Jack Lucas would be awake along with Cavazos and he wouldn't have much to worry about. Maybe he could get a few hour's sleep.

"Who put you in charge here instead of him?"

Cavazos asked, dislike all over him. "We did not even stand watch the other time." Joe had been correct in his assumption.

"Mr. Winston Haverty put me in charge," Joe answered patiently, a tight smile pulling at his mouth. "What was done the other time has already happened. This is a different time. I don't want anything happening to us or the cattle. I don't want anything especially to happen to me."

Joe and Cavazos stared at each other intently. The army scout knew that it wouldn't take much for the dark-skinned man to come at him. There was a challenge in Joe's brown eyes.

Muttering something in Spanish which was probably an oath and questioning the species of Joe's mother, Cavazos took a rifle from the scabbard on his saddle and walked in hard steps a little away from the camp.

"Do you think you can stay awake as long as he's on watch?" Joe asked Lucas in a whisper as Cavazos walked away. "I don't trust him."

"Oh, sure," Lucas answered, putting more coffee grounds and water into the blackened pot on the rock by the fire. "I don't trust him any more than you do. He and Graff were very friendly last month. I think they had some kind of plan in mind for this trip. That's one reason why he's been so tacky to you." Lucas narrowed his eyes and pulled his mouth into a thin line. Joe couldn't help but roar in laughter at the word.

"I don't care how 'tacky' he is to me," Joe said, clearing his throat and swallowing a mouthful of coffee, "just as long as he doesn't try to kill me."

Joe stretched out on the ground, pulling his hat down over his face and the extra blanket up over his shoulders. He knew that it was unlikely that he would get any sleep. There were too many things on his mind for that. He trusted Jack Lucas. Maybe he would be able to get some sleep.

One of the Mexicans took out a harmonica and the last thing that Joe Howard remembered hearing, amid the night sounds and the wind, was a soft melancholy tune.

Joe was awakened by a hand shaking his shoulder. He was relieved and a little surprised to see Jack Lucas bending over him. Joe had been almost certain that Armando Cavazos would have tried to kill him.

"Did you have any trouble out of anyone?" Joe asked in a low voice as he stood up and stretched.

"No," Lucas answered, dropping down on his bedroll. "Cavazos hasn't said a word all night. I think he was a little irritated that I didn't go to sleep. Maybe he thinks that I stayed awake just to keep an eye on him."

Joe changed his mind a little about Ranger Jack Lucas. Keeping an eye on Armando Cavazos was exactly what Joe had wanted him to do. Joe settled the Colt .45 more comfortably around his waist as he walked a short distance from the sleeping men on the ground. He counted five shapes on the ground besides Lucas and knew that Cavazos was where he should be.

Walking over to where the cows were milling around or bedding down, Joe thought about Chief

Keoni and the kind of meat that he was getting. There wouldn't be enough meat on those hundred cows to last Keoni's people until the cooking water got hot. He thought about his plan and could feel a smile easing across his mouth. Maybe soon, Joe thought grimly, if I have my way about this, things will change for the better for the bronze-skinned man and his people.

Whoever was getting these cattle was a lot better off than Keoni but not quite so much as Senator Caleb Powers. Joe couldn't wait until he got back to the fort and could tell Eric McRaney about this. It would definitely be another reason for McRaney to dislike Powers and maybe he would go after him himself. The senator was violating a government treaty and he could be arrested. Joe shivered as a good feeling crept through his bones.

But, Joe thought pragmatically as he started back to camp, Powers really hadn't done anything illegal if he had bought the herd of cattle from Bruell. It would only have been illegal if he took the herd of cattle without paying for it. Joe knew that he would have to get a closer look at the ledger in Winston Haverty's office. Maybe he would find the name of the third recipient of cattle.

Joe was almost to the camp when he heard a low moan, a thud, and running footsteps. Jerking the Colt .45 from the holster, he bent low in a walking crouch and eased forward. There wasn't enough light from the rising moon to see anything out of the ordinary. He could still make out the six men on the ground and assumed that all of them were sleeping.

My mind and ears must be playing tricks on me, Joe thought as he stood up and reholstered the pistol. Maybe one of the men was having a bad dream. Maybe some animal had made the running sound. Deciding that that was what had caused the noise, Joe relaxed a little and watched the yellow ball in the east clear the horizon to begin its ride across the dark sky where millions and millions of stars twinkled.

It's too bad a man's life has to be so complicated, Joe thought, taking a deep lung full of the crisp, clean-smelling air. It's so unlike the stars. All a star has to do is twinkle so beautifully at night.

There were so many things racing around in Joe's mind that he wasn't aware that a thin line of pink had begun separating the earth from the sky. Dawn was already breaking.

Standing up, Joe kicked his legs out to get rid of the cramps and started back toward the camp. He had expected to smell coffee bubbling on the fire, but there was nothing going on.

Jack Lucas was still lying on the ground with the drab gray blanket up around his shoulders. His hat was over his face. Joe looked over to where the Mexicans had spread their blankets. A hard knot pulled in his stomach when he counted only three men. Looking closely at them, his heart began pounding faster when he realized that Armando Cavazos and the tall Mexican were missing. Then Joe remembered the odd sounds from last night.

Turning quickly back to Jack Lucas, Joe bent down to shake him awake. When Joe touched Lucas's shoulder, the hat fell away and Joe couldn't

110

believe what he saw. His stomach turned over and he wanted to vomit.

Jack Lucas's throat had been slit from one ear to the other. Blood was caked all over the front of his light blue shirt and on the top part of the blanket. Standing up, Joe took a couple of stumbling steps backward and had to swallow hard several times to keep the contents of his stomach in place.

He would curse himself for the rest of his life for not checking on the strange sounds last night. But, he wondered, feeling his stomach turn over again, why had Armando Cavazos killed Jack Lucas? They had worked together before and there hadn't seemed to be any bad feelings between the two men. Joe had been the one having all the trouble with the Mexican. Joe wondered why Cavazos hadn't killed him last night. He certainly had had the opportunity.

Walking as quietly and quickly as he could over to the sleeping Mexicans, Joe drew the Colt .45 and pulled the hammer back. He wondered why they hadn't gone with the other two men.

"Despierte. Su habla Ingles?" Joe shouted in a loud voice. Apparently these three sleeping men weren't as loyal or important to Armando Cavazos as the tall Mexican was. But why had they been left behind? They could identify the other two men. Joe knew beyond a shadow of a doubt that Cavazos had killed Lucas, but why? His quarrel had been with Joe—why hadn't Cavazos killed *him?* Cavazos had had an opportunity to kill Joe last night. The intent had been alive in his black eyes all along. Joe had been far enough away from the camp for Cavazos to

111

have killed him, and the Mexican would have nothing to lose. Why hadn't Cavazos taken the cattle? These questions would bother Joe for a long time.

"Yes, we understand you," the older-looking one of the three said, getting slowly to his feet. He never took his uncertain, fearful dark eyes off Joe.

"What is your name and who did that?" Joe asked in a cold voice, breathing hard. He jerked his thumb over his shoulder at the lifeless body on the ground. As soon as Joe asked the question, he felt stupid. Armando Cavazos had killed Jack Lucas for some strange reason. Was it to get back at Joe for something? Somehow he doubted it.

"Armando killed him," the man answered, his black eyes getting bigger and bigger. "My name is Rique Sanchez." He glanced nervously from one man to the other. "That is Juan Gonzales, and the other is Tomas Mendoza. What are you going to do?"

They crossed themselves.

Joe had a decision to make. Should he bury Jack Lucas out here in the middle of nowhere or take him all the way into Brewster? There was still another day's ride left. It was July and the sun would have no mercy on anything that walked, crawled, or flew too close to the ground. The decision was made for Joe in a matter of seconds. He would have to bury Lucas out here. But since there was nothing to use to dig a grave, they would just have to cover him with rocks. That would be no problem. There were enough rocks on the ground to build a house.

It didn't take long for the four men to bury Jack Lucas with enough rocks that no predators would bother him for a long time. Joe had looked in Lucas's pockets for some identification. The only thing he found was Lucas's name on a tattered piece of paper, ten dollars in bills, and thirty-five cents in change. There was nothing to indicate that he had been a Texas Ranger. A staggering thought hit Joe Howard right between the eyes. Maybe Lucas wasn't a Ranger after all. Joe only had his word that he was. Could Jack Lucas have been the one to get the cows in Brewster? He would find out about that tonight or tomorrow night at the latest. But there was one other place that Joe could look for some identification for Jack Lucas. Walking over to the dead man's saddlebags, he dug deep and felt ashamed when his fingers curled around something metal and pointed. Withdrawing his hand, Joe looked down at his hand. In it was a star with the words TEXAS RANGER on it. Joe put the star back into the saddlebag and stood up.

"Do you have any idea where they would have gone?" Joe asked, looking at Sanchez. The man was about Joe's height, with a couple more pounds on him. He appeared as confused as Joe felt.

"No," Sanchez answered, shaking his head slowly. "And that is the truth," Sanchez quickly added when Joe gave him a skeptical look.

"Well," Joe said, knowing that it would do no good to argue with the man, "let's spread out and see if we can find any tracks."

Joe knew that it would be a waste of time and energy to look for tracks since so much time had already passed since Jack Lucas had been killed. But he felt that he had to make the gesture.

113

He was puzzled when he found tracks leading out toward Brewster, if that was where they were heading. But that didn't necessarily mean that Brewster was where Cavazos and the other man were going.

"What is the other man's name?" Joe asked as they gathered their gear and mounted up.

"His name is Gilbert Romay," Sanchez answered, pulling his horse up by Joe. "He and Armando have been good friends for a long time."

The four men pressed the cattle into a tighter herd and started toward Brewster.

The sun had about two hours left when they reached the holding pens north of town. They were empty, as Joe had expected. A young boy was there putting out hay when they arrived. Joe didn't think that anyone would come for the cattle before night. That would give Joe enough time to find the sheriff, tell him what had happened, and find a place to hide and watch the pens to see who showed up. But he saw a boulder about a hundred feet from the back of the pens and decided that would be an ideal place to hide.

The sheriff's office was at the edge of town. Joe wondered if he should tell the sheriff who he was as he dismounted and tied Serge to the hitch rail. He decided not to. He didn't know who was and wasn't involved in the deal here in Brewster.

"I am Joe Howard," he said to the big, burly, black-haired man sitting behind a desk with a six-pronged star pinned on the left pocket of his gray shirt. "Six other men and I brought a herd of cattle in from Marathon to here. Last night Armando Cavazos

114

killed Jack Lucas. Then Cavazos and Gilbert Romay left. We buried Lucas about ten miles back. I thought that you should know about it. He was a Texas Ranger."

Joe was suddenly aware of the indifferent look on the sheriff's wide, ruddy face, and he realized that he was rambling on so fast that all of his words were running together.

"Hold on a minute. Slow down," the sheriff said in a raspy voice, raising his hand to stop Joe's rapid inarticulate explanation. "I'm Sheriff Pierce Jagger and the next train doesn't come through here until noon so you have plenty of time to start from the beginning."

The sheriff leaned back in an armed chair with a high back, peaked his fingers together, tilted his head to the right, and seemed ready to hear Joe's story.

Joe started from the beginning, hitting the high spots and leaving out the fact that he was an army scout from Fort Davis. He watched impatiently as skepticism and suspicion narrowed Jagger's slate-green eyes.

"Now tell me why I should believe you," Jagger said, blinking his heavy eyelids slowly. "There has been a herd of cattle coming in here every month or so for the past year and there hasn't been any report of any kind of trouble up until now." Jagger looked up at Joe, a miscreant smile on his thick mouth.

Joe stood dumbfounded in front of the cluttered desk and knew that he was probably staring at the sheriff.

"Well, there's a first time for everything, sheriff,"

Joe said candidly, taking a deep breath. "Aren't you going to do anything? Aren't you even going to question the three men who were with me? They stopped at a cantina down the street." He gestured with his left arm in the direction from which he'd just come. He'd thought that at the very mention of a man being killed in such a brutal way and having the name of the killer that the sheriff would at least fill out some kind of paper and probably look around town for Armando Cavazos and Gilbert Romay. Neither of the two men would be hard to find. Armando Cavazos with his build and Gilbert Romay with his thin height would stand out like a red bean in a spoon of sugar.

But evidently none of that was going to happen. Sheriff Pierce Jagger made no move to get up. Instead he slid down in the chair and crossed his legs. "Ten miles back isn't in my jurisdiction," Jagger said, a defiant expression in his eyes. He shook his head slowly. A stillness settled over his wide face.

Joe couldn't believe what he was hearing. The ten miles back was a lot closer to Brewster than it was to Marathon and it seemed to him that the sheriff should have wanted to go out there out of curiosity if nothing else.

"But you're the sheriff here!" Joe insisted, leaning over and bracing hands palms down on the edge of the desk. "We couldn't bring the body in and it's too far to go back to Marathon."

"The ten miles out isn't in my jurisdiction," Jagger repeated, an evident warning in his eyes and voice.

Joe suddenly realized that he was wasting his time and breath. He suspected that if he'd told Jagger that this particular killing had taken place right in front of the jail, it wouldn't have been in his jurisdiction. Sheriff Jagger had to be involved some way with Winston Haverty and Armando Cavazos. More questions to be answered.

Knowing that time was passing by, Joe shook his head in disgust, pulling his hat down low on his forehead, and stomped out of the jail, slamming the door shut behind him.

Jack Lucas had told Joe that as soon as he, Graff, and the other men had left the cattle at the holding pens the last time, they'd left without waiting around to see who would come to claim them.

Determined to find out who the second person would be, Joe had to get back to the boulders that would offer a hiding place at the holding pens and settle in. The three Mexicans, since their job was finished, were nowhere in sight when Joe left the jail. He'd thought that they would be waiting for him when he came out. He'd thought that they would hurry and have a beer and come to hear what the sheriff had to say. He wondered where Armando Cavazos and Gilbert Romay were as he stopped by the livery to water Serge and the bay that had belonged to Jack Lucas and to fill his canteen. He left the bay at the livery to pick up later.

Long shadows, cast by the granite mountains and boulders, were crawling eastward across the ground when Joe arrived back at the holding pen. The boy was gone and the only sounds came from the cattle,

117

the wind, and a few birds chirping in nearby oak trees.

Joe didn't have any idea which direction whoever owned the cows would come from. He knew that he was taking a big risk no matter where he chose to hide and decided against the boulder. That was too close and on the ground. He would need a higher vantage point. He picked a spot on a high ridge about a hundred and fifty feet away. There was an outcropping that would provide a little shade for him and Serge.

Having no idea how long he'd have to wait, Joe unsaddled Serge, then sat down and leaned back against the saddle. He was made aware of how long it had been since he'd eaten anything when a rumbling sounded in his stomach. There was some jerky in the saddlebags and that would have to do until his curiosity was satisfied. He hoped that whoever was going to show up would do it before dark.

No more than twenty minutes had passed when the partial stillness was broken by hoofbeats on the rocks and hard-packed ground below. Rising to a low squat, Joe wasn't really prepared for what he saw. Riding slowly and looking around in all directions was none other than Armando Cavazos! But he was alone. Joe wondered where Gilbert Romay was. Maybe Cavazos had killed him.

Joe stood up for a better look around and made the mistake of not watching where he moved his foot. The toe of his boot dislodged a rock and sent it rolling down the slope. That same rock caused a small avalanche of pebbles, rocks, and sand.

Armando Cavazos heard the commotion, looked up, and saw Joe standing on the ridge. Pulling a rifle from the scabbard, Cavazos put it up to his shoulder, slammed a shell in the chamber, and squeezed the trigger. The bullet plowed into the ground fifty feet below where Joe was standing.

Joe was irritated at his thoughtlessness in unsaddling Serge and not taking his rifle out of the scabbard. Joe knew he couldn't get Cavazos with a pistol from this distance, so he spun around, jerked the Winchester from its scabbard in the saddle on the ground, took aim, and fired. Cavazos, anticipating Joe's action, had spurred his horse forward out of reach. The bullet stirred up the dust just behind the horse.

Joe wished again that he hadn't unsaddled Serge. There wasn't time to put the saddle back on. He'd have to ride bareback if he was going to catch Cavazos.

Swinging up on Serge's broad back, Joe looked down the slope and saw Cavazos disappearing behind a rise. Riding halfway down, Joe pulled Serge to a stop and dismounted.

Tying Serge to a small scrub bush, Joe eased around and started climbing up the opposite way. He stopped when he was about twenty feet away from a boulder that was about ten feet tall. Looking down at the ground, he saw hoofprints going up and knew that Armando Cavazos couldn't be too far away.

Joe wondered if the big Mexican would go on up to the top of the ridge and wait in ambush for him or if he'd ride down the opposite way and try to come up behind him.

But it didn't happen that way. Holding the Winchester at hip level, Joe stood listening. He felt as if he were in no-man's land when he didn't hear anything. He stepped away from the boulder and almost dropped the Winchester in surprise when he looked Armando Cavazos straight in the eye! Each man was caught off guard at the other's sudden appearance. Cavazos had his rifle up to his shoulder and aimed directly at Joe's head. But Joe's reflexes were a little faster and he got off the first and better shot.

The bullet couldn't have missed such a big target and at so close a range. It tore into the center of Cavazos's yellow shirt, and blood began oozing from the hold. Cavazos's knees began sagging as he dropped the rifle and started clawing at his chest with his cigar-sized fingers. His still hate-filled black eyes closed, then opened one more time before closing as he hit the ground on his back. A shuddering breath hissed through his teeth, then he lay still. Armando Cavazos was dead.

Bending down, Joe picked up the rifle and stuck it under his arm. There wasn't time to bury Cavazos right then and Joe felt bad for a short while when he walked all the way around the boulder and found the dead man's horse. Gathering up the reins, he led the horse back to where Serge was tied, swung up, and rode back to the ridge. He wondered why Armando Cavazos had come back to the cattle pens. Had he come back to meet someone or was he just making sure the cattle had arrived?

Dismounting, Joe only loosened the cinch on

Serge this time and sat down to wait again. A gut feeling told him that Armando Cavazos wasn't the only one he was really waiting for. It had to be someone more important.

The sun was just going down behind a mountain, shrouding it with red and gold colors, when once again Joe heard approaching horses. There was still enough light for Joe to only have to squint a little to see Winston Haverty and Bernie Graff riding slowly toward the holding pen.

Winston Haverty and Bernie Graff! Joe was and wasn't surprised that Winston Haverty was the one to get the cattle here in Brewster. He was surprised, though, that Bernie Graff was with him. Graff was supposed to be taking the other cattle to Marfa with Miles Rymer. How had he gotten back so fast? He couldn't have. He had probably never left Marathon. Haverty had just wanted everyone to think that he had. Joe wondered why Graff was here and he also wondered who was helping Miles Rymer.

Joe watched the two men dismount and tie their horses to the log fence beside a water trough. He was too far away to hear what they were saying, but evidently they were going to wait for someone because they took the water canteens from the saddles and walked over and sat down under a small oak tree.

Darkness soon spread over the land and it didn't take long for the night sounds to begin drifting across the vastness on a cooling wind. Joe got hungry again and finished chewing on the piece of jerky.

Finally using the security of the darkness, Joe,

being more careful now where he put his feet and glad once again that he'd never gotten in the habit of wearing spurs, circled down to the right of the cattle pen, and all the way around it. He wanted to get close enough to the two men to hear what they were saying. It was obvious that they were waiting for someone, but who? It had to be Armando Cavazos. He was the only one who had been there. Apparently there hadn't been a definite meeting time.

Joe knew that his presence wouldn't bother the cattle too much, and even if it did, maybe Haverty and Graff would think that it was only an animal moving around. Easing as close as he could, Joe was surprised and dismayed at what he heard.

"What do you think is keeping Cavazos so long?" Winston Haverty asked Bernie Graff. He removed the cap from his water canteen and took a long swig. He looked like a kid sitting there on the ground by the big man.

"I don't know," Graff replied, stretching out his long legs, which looked like small tree trunks. "He should have had plenty of time to be here by now. All he and Gilbert Romay had to do was kill that Texas Ranger."

Joe Howard was sure that the air he'd sucked in through his teeth in a shocked gasp could be heard all the way into Marathon. He froze in his squatting position behind Graff and Haverty.

How on earth had Winston Haverty and Bernie Graff known that Jack Lucas was a Texas Ranger? How long had they known it? Had they intended for Cavazos to kill him also? Or did they really think that he was just a stupid saddle bum riding through Marathon?

"You know," Haverty said reflectively, pushing his tan hat back on his yellow head, "our little setup here could have really been messed up if Sheriff Pierce Jagger hadn't recognized Jack Lucas as a Texas Ranger when you two came to Brewster last month. Jagger already knew that you were working for me and put everything together."

Joe was glad now that he hadn't told Jagger that he was an army scout. He expelled a deep breath as he understood why the sheriff hadn't shown any interest or surprise when Joe had told him that Jack Lucas had been killed or who had done it. Joe also understood why Jagger wasn't surprised when Joe had told him that Lucas was a Ranger. The sheriff was in on the whole thing.

Joe wondered how many cows Sheriff Pierce Jagger would get for his part in the deal. Joe knew that the Indians needed the cattle a lot more than Jagger did. At that very minute, Joe Howard wanted to kill Winston Haverty so badly that it was all that he could do to keep from pulling the .45 from the holster and fulfilling that desire. But he knew that he couldn't do that if he wanted to tie Senator Caleb Powers into all of this.

"What are you going to do about this new guy, this Joe Howard?" Graff asked, hostility in his voice.

"Oh, he'll probably want to be long gone after he's paid," Haverty said, a chuckle in his voice. "Why?"

"Oh, there's something strange about him," Graff answered, crossing his legs at the ankles. "I just don't think he's who he claims to be either. He asks too many questions and has a way of being everywhere at the same time."

"Ah, don't worry about him," Haverty said, reaching out and slapping the big man on the shoulder. "You just don't like him because he laughed at your name and hit you with a currycomb. He's just a stupid saddle bum. He'll be gone before long."

Just a stupid saddle bum, huh, Joe thought, a hard knot working in his lean jaw. We'll see who's a stupid saddle bum!

"How much longer are we going to wait for them?" Graff asked, standing up and stretching.

"Not any longer," Haverty said, getting to his feet with a grunt. "We'll spend the night here in Brewster. Maybe Cavazos and Romay will show up at the hotel later. We can load the cows on the train for Chicago in the morning."

"Where do you think Howard and the other three Mexicans went?" Graff asked as they started toward their horses.

"Maybe Cavazos and Romay killed them," Haverty suggested with smugness in his voice. "Even if Howard did tell the sheriff what had happened," Haverty continued, swinging up on the McClellan saddle, "Jagger won't do anything. Those four would be just as well off if they were in a saloon getting drunk."

Joe Howard was being eaten up with rage as he retraced his steps back to Serge and Cavazos's horse. Two ideas popped into his mind. Maybe he could do them both tonight.

He hadn't thought about Haverty moving the cattle by rail and hadn't taken the time even to see if a train ran through the town. If that were the case, the tracks would have to be north of Brewster and the cattle would have to be driven a little way.

When Haverty had said that the cattle were going to Chicago, Joe knew immediately what was happening. Haverty was selling cattle that he'd gotten for nothing to buyers or packing houses in the East. Joe wished now that he'd gone ahead and killed him and Bernie Graff when he'd had the chance a few minutes ago.

Chapter 5

Darkness enveloped the land like a soft glove as Joe Howard rode back toward Brewster. Winston Haverty had given him an idea and it would help put his plans into motion.

On the way into town earlier, Joe had seen the small cantina. Being sure that neither Winston Haverty nor Bernie Graff would frequent such a place, Joe tied both horses to the loose hitch rail and opened the squeaky-hinged batwings. This was where the three Mexicans would probably still be if they hadn't already left town.

The small place was packed. Men were standing almost jowl-to-jowl at the bar. The air was thick with cigar and cigarette smoke, the fragrance or odor, depending on how one wanted to look at it, of cheap perfume, and a mixture of spicy food aromas. Joe had to blink his smarting eyes a couple of times before he was able to see anything.

When his eyes finally cleared, Joe looked around.

He grinned when he saw Rique Sanchez, Juan Gonzales, and Tomas Mendoza sitting in the rear left corner sharing one bottle of tequila. They were deeply engrossed in an animated conversation and almost jumped out of their clothes when Joe walked up to them.

"Have you men eaten yet?" Joe asked, putting his hand on Sanchez's shoulder. Their horses must have been tied out back and he hadn't seen them.

"No," Sanchez answered, his black eyes wide in real fear as he glanced quickly from Joe to Gonzales, then over to Mendoza and finally back up at Joe.

"Mind if I join you?" Joe asked, removing his hand from Sanchez's shoulder and taking hold of the back of a rickety chair. Unsure how the three men would react to him, he waited until all three of them nodded. Turning around, he motioned for a waiter, pulled out the chair and sat down, then expelled a long, deep breath.

Joe was so hungry he'd eat just about anything, and he told the waiter to bring him a plate full of whatever was in the kitchen. The waiter glanced at his three kinsmen and grinned deviously. Joe, catching the interchange of looks, knew what they were plotting and braced himself for probably some of the hottest food that he would ever eat.

When the waiter returned, he was carrying four plates, all filled with the same thing: tortillas, chili, beans, and tamales. On each plate were two green peppers. Joe knew what he had to do and decided to go ahead and get it done. Postponing the inevitable would probably only make the peppers hotter.

The three Mexicans seemed to be looking down at their plates as they dug into the food. But Joe knew that they were watching to see what he would do with his peppers. Bracing himself against the impending heat, he picked up a pepper and bit into it.

Almost instantly heat filled his mouth, the end of his tongue caught fire, and he was sure his teeth were going to melt. Joe was positive that if he expelled a breath, red flame would shoot out of his mouth. He tried to act nonchalant as he cut off a piece of tamale and put it in his mouth. That absorbed only about a tenth of the heat and Joe felt a tear roll down his face. He picked up the full mug of beer, downed it in a couple of gulps, slammed the mug down on the table, and expelled a breath that would warm the entire place. Taking another deep breath, Joe swallowed hard and looked at each of the Mexicans, a see-I-did-it look in his smarting eyes.

The three men threw back their heads and their admiring laughter filled the place. The four men finished eating and asked for beer refills. Joe didn't finish the peppers. He felt that he'd proven his point.

"How would you men like to go on a long ride?" Joe asked, leaning back in the chair, a challenge gleaming in his narrowed eyes, which had finally stopped watering.

"Doing what and going where?" Rique Sanchez asked, losing a little of his subservience. A small, skeptical frown pulled between his black brows.

"You know that Winston Haverty has been sending the Indians at Elephant Mountain bad meat," Joe said, leaning forward and resting his elbows on the table. The three men nodded. "Haverty has a hundred healthy cows out there in that pen. Haverty, Graff, and Cavazos have been in on this deal all along."

Joe was really surprised when the three men looked at each other in shock.

"Have you seen Armando Cavazos here in town?" Tomas Mendoza asked, looking over at Joe.

"I killed him on a ridge at the cattle pens about three hours ago," Joe said, watching a different kind of expression take place in their eyes. It seemed to be one of genuine respect.

"You killed Armando Cavazos?" Juan Gonzales asked, drawing the words out slowly as he leaned forward and stared at Joe. There was disbelief all over his face.

"It was either him or me," Joe replied wearily, nodding his head. The Mexicans' eyes would never be that wide again.

"What do you want us to do?" Sanchez asked, excitement sparkling in his eyes.

"We are going to take something from someone who more or less stole it from someone who really needs it." Joe would have been greatly disappointed if shock and bewilderment hadn't raced across the three men's faces.

"What are you talking about?" Sanchez asked, leaning back in the chair as if to escape Joe. "Isn't stealing supposed to be a little dishonest?" There was a little sarcasm and a lot of trepidation in his eyes and voice.

"Stealing is taking something that belongs to

someone," Joe explained, nodding his head resolutely. The three men watched him without saying anything but expectancy was all over their faces.

"We're going to take twenty of those cows and drive them to Chief Keoni and his people at Elephant Mountain." The plan sounded so simple to Joe and in his mind he could actually see it working.

The three Mexican's reaction would probably have been no different if he'd told them that he was going to push them, totally naked, from the top of a building.

"We can't do that," Sanchez argued, shaking his head and leaning forward to glare at Joe.

"Oh, yes we can," Joe insisted stoically, smiling shrewdly, a cunning in his eyes. "Those Indians are starving to death. They can't eat the rotten meat that Haverty has been sending to them for the past couple of months. What would you do if your family was hungry? What would you do if you were supposed to be getting good food and only ended up with something that even a dog wouldn't eat?"

Joe thought that he had been speaking quietly and hadn't realized that his voice had risen until he saw Sanchez glancing nervously around. Joe looked over his shoulder and was embarrassed to see several men watching him.

Turning back around in the chair, Joe thought that if he appealed to their sympathetic side, the three men would be more willing to help him. He knew he was on the right track when a remorseful expression crept into their dark eyes.

"I would not like that," Sanchez said woefully,

shaking his head regretfully. The other two men looked at Sanchez and nodded. Sanchez raised his head and held Joe's gaze for a long time.

"Will you help me?" Joe asked, knowing deep inside him that they would give in and do it. "You know that I'm going to do it with or without your help. It would be a lot easier if you were along." They hesitated. "I'll pay each of you a dollar."

The three men exchanged looks again before glancing at Joe. Then they smiled and slowly nodded in agreement.

"Do you know when Winston Haverty and Bernie Graff are coming back for the cattle?" Mendoza asked, picking up his big tan sombrero from the floor and plopping it down on his head. The four men stood up and put money down on the table for their meal. Sanchez, Gonzales, and Joe had kept their hats on.

"I heard Haverty say that if Cavazos didn't come to the hotel tonight," Joe said, swinging up on Serge, "that they would put the cows on a train in the morning for Chicago. So we should have plenty of time to get the cattle a good distance away from here by then."

Joe could detect a different attitude in the men's eyes in the light from the cantina. They were as excited as he was nervous. This was stealing and the first illegal thing that he had ever done in his life. No matter how he had tried to rationalize what they were about to do, it was still stealing.

But he really wasn't too bothered about it and was sure that his conscience would be able to cope with it.

To know that Keoni and his people were eating good meat would be worth any trouble he would encounter. Something told him that that would be a lot if Winston Haverty and Bernie Graff caught up with them.

When they passed the livery stable, Joe got the horses that had belonged to Jack Lucas and Armando Cavazos. He wondered if Winston Haverty would go back and put a guard at the cattle pens but doubted it, probably thinking that Cavazos would finally show up.

"Why didn't you three men leave when Armando Cavazos and Gilbert Romay killed Jack Lucas?" Joe asked Sanchez when he rode up beside him.

"We didn't know that he had been killed until you woke us up," Sanchez answered, shrugging his shoulders and arching his black brows.

"Did you know that Lucas was a Texas Ranger?" Joe asked. He could tell instantly from the shocked look on Sanchez's face that he didn't before he shook his head.

"What did you do with Cavazos's body?" Sanchez asked when they reached the cattle pens.

"He's up there in the rocks," Joe answered, a sinister grin pulling at the corner of his mouth. He indicated the direction with a jab of his thumb toward the ridge. "After we get the cattle started, I'm going to bring it down here." He wondered if he'd be able to get the big man's body up on a horse by himself.

"Since you say that we're not stealing," Mendoza said, riding up by Joe at the gate, "why are we going to waste our time with twenty cows when we can take the entire herd. They probably belong to the Indians anyway."

"I like the way you think," Joe said, reaching out and slapping him on the shoulder. "We'll do it." Joe knew that if they hadn't suggested it, he would have done it anyway.

Tomas Mendoza opened the gate while Joe, Sanchez, and Gonzales rode into the pen and drove the cows out. It didn't take much to get them headed south. Handing Mendoza the reins of Jack's horse, Joe led Cavazos's horse up on the ridge, dismounted, and using every muscle in his body and some he didn't know he had, put the big Mexican's body on the skittish horse, went back to the cattle pen, pulled the body from the horse unceremoniously and let it drop in front of the open gate. He wished he could have stayed around to see how Winston Haverty and Bernie Graff would react when they came back for the cattle. Joe wondered how long it would take for Haverty to figure out that he was the one who had killed Armando Cavazos. Something told him that he hadn't seen the last of Winston Haverty. The man might be small but he wasn't stupid.

It didn't take long to catch up with Sanchez, Gonzales, and Mendoza. As the four men rode along in the night, Joe couldn't help glancing over his shoulder from time to time. He knew that Haverty wasn't likely to miss the cattle until early morning, but the short hairs on the back of his neck kept standing up and he'd learned a long time ago not to ignore the warning.

134

Joe had never driven cattle at night but apparently the three Mexicans and he suspected, no matter what Sanchez had said to the contrary about stealing, that all those drives hadn't been legal.

When he suggested that they stop and make camp for the night, Sanchez insisted that they go on a little farther. Maybe they were afraid that Haverty and Graff would catch up with them if they stopped so close so soon.

Knowing that it would be at least a three-day ride to Elephant Mountain, even with this much time ahead of them, Joe began doubting the merit of his decision. But it was too late to turn back now. Deep inside he knew that he was doing the right thing.

The moon was a bright yellow ball directly overhead when Joe called a halt for the night. He and the others had been up since early that morning, and if they were like him, they were bone tired and hungry. A lot had happened to him and it was finally getting to him.

Joe wasn't going to waste time with a bedroll in case they had to move in a hurry. He only loosened the cinch on the saddle, then dropped down on the ground and leaned up against a boulder. Mendoza offered to stand guard for a while.

"Do you know a man named Silas Bruell?" Joe asked Rique Sanchez when he sat down on the ground by him.

"Yes," Sanchez answered, expelling a deep and tired breath. "He is the white man who sold Winston Haverty the cattle."

"Do you know where Bruell got the cattle?" Joe

asked, remembering that Jack Lucas had said something about rustled cattle.

"No," Sanchez answered, trying to stifle a yawn. He took off his big hat, rolled it up, stuck it under his head, and stretched out on the ground. It wasn't long before he was snoring.

"Do you know where Bruell lives?" Joe asked, trying hard to keep his own eyes open. Getting up, he got the coffeepot, water, and coffee. Gonzales saw what he was doing and made a small fire before answering Joe's question.

"He lives in San Angelo," Gonzales said, sitting down after taking a cup from his saddlebag.

"Why didn't you all leave after we buried Lucas this morning?" Joe asked, remembering that Winston Haverty had told him that Ed Spencer had gone to San Angelo. Was Spencer going for more cattle?

Joe saw Gonzales grin at him in the flickering firelight. "That's the first thing I would have done," Joe said.

"We were hired to do a job," Gonzales replied, shrugging his shoulders. "We had not gotten the cattle to the pen."

A look in Gonzales's black eyes dared Joe to argue with him but there was no way in the world that Joe Howard was going to believe that line. He gave his head a quick jerk and looked away.

Joe's mind was in a whirl. There were too many names and too many places to keep straight. Marfa. Marathon. Elephant Mountain. Alpine and Fort Davis. Senator Caleb Powers. Winston Haverty. Silas Bruell. Bernie Graff. Chief Keoni and Colonel Eric

McRaney. He hoped that all this came together before his brain exploded.

Joe realized he needed some help. Since Senator Caleb Powers was involved in this now, it had become the government's business. Joe decided after they delivered the cattle to the Indians, he would go back to Fort Davis and tell Colonel McRaney the whole story.

With that thought in mind, Joe downed his cup of hot coffee, stretched out on the ground, and went to sleep, leaving Gonzales to put out the fire.

Joe woke up when the first hint of daylight was touching the eastern sky. The four men took only enough time to make coffee before starting the cattle toward Elephant Mountain again. Joe guessed that by now Winston Haverty and Bernie Graff knew that the cattle were gone. He wondered what Haverty had done when he saw Armando Cavazos's body. If he'd been in Winston Haverty's well-made boots, Joe would have figured out instantly what had happened and wouldn't waste time coming after the cows and whoever had taken them.

Joe was glad now that Sanchez had insisted they ride long after it was dark last night. He was curious to know how close Haverty and Graff were. Handing Serge's reins to Mendoza, Joe tightened the cinch on Lucas's horse and swung up. The bay was rested and it didn't take long for him to ride up on a mesa, which provided a view for miles in all directions. Opening the saddlebags, he took out a pair of binoculars, put them up to his eyes, and wasn't disappointed to see a dust cloud coming from the north. From the looks of it, there were more than two riders. Two horses couldn't raise that much dust.

Turning the horse around, Joe slammed his heels in its sides. "We've got to move these cows a little faster," Joe yelled out to Sanchez, who was riding at the back of the herd. "Haverty and probably several others are about half a day's ride away."

Sanchez looked noncommitally at Joe, nodded, and without saying anything, pulled a huge pistol from the holster, raised it high over his head, and fired two quick shots into the air. The sound startled the cattle and Sanchez got the action he wanted. The herd started running and covered a lot more ground than they would have otherwise.

They let the cows go at this pace until they reached a small stream. They would have had to slow down to cross it anyway and took time to make coffee and cook something to eat. Joe put the binoculars in his saddlebags.

Deciding to ride back for another look, Joe swung up on Serge, rode up on a bluff, and couldn't believe his eyes. Winston Haverty, Bernie Graff, and the others were much closer than Joe had anticipated. They must have been pushing their mounts as fast as Joe and the three Mexicans were pushing their horses and the cattle. The riders were only a couple of miles away! They must not have stopped to eat.

Swinging Serge around, Joe raced back to the stream. Sanchez could tell from the look on Joe's face that something was wrong.

"*Que pasa?*" Sanchez asked in Spanish, although he'd been using English before. He pulled his horse to a stop and waited for Joe to catch up. Maybe he didn't want to waste time struggling for the question in English.

"Haverty and Graff are only a couple of miles behind us," Joe said, breathing heavily as he hauled back on the reins. "We've got to find a place for these cattle until later. Do you know of a place?"

In rapid Spanish, and Joe couldn't catch a single word, Sanchez spoke to Mendoza and Gonzales. A thoughtful frown pulled lines between both mens' brows. Suddenly Mendoza stiffened in the saddle, relaxed, and smiled. Motioning forward with his right arm, he led the way to an arroyo that widened with walls on the east end too tall for a cow to climb. That would do to hold the cattle, but the men would be sitting ducks!

"We can't do this," Joe shouted as he rode out of the arroyo. "We have to get up to a higher place." The Mexicans looked around them and suddenly realized what a predicament they would be in if they didn't get out of there fast.

A ridge about three hundred yards away with an outcropping would serve the purpose if they could get there in time. But Winston Haverty or someone with him either knew of the place or had seen it. Two rifle shots rang out as Joe and Sanchez reached the top. There was no vegetation on the ridge and only boulders offered any protection. Six men, counting Graff, were with Haverty. Joe dismounted and eased to the edge of the outcropping. Just as he looked over, another shot rang out. He had just enough time to peep over and count seven horses below before the bullet whizzed past.

In a squatting walk, Joe got back to Serge, pulled his rifle from the scabbard, and dropped down behind a boulder as he heard footsteps coming up the side. The footsteps stopped and Joe wondered where the man was. He started to move out a little to see but paused when he heard a noise on the boulder above him.

Joe's heart skipped a beat as he looked up. One of Winston Haverty's men was standing there, a Henry rifle aimed directly down at him, his finger on the trigger.

The saying that one never hears the shot that kills him popped into Joe's mind as he heard a pistol explode a few feet behind him. He looked around, then back at the man standing above him. He had dropped the rifle and was now clutching the front of his blue shirt with both hands. A red stain was spreading across the front of it. A look of disbelief was in the man's wide eyes. His knees began sagging and he fell over with a thud almost at Joe's feet. Joe looked back around to his left and saw Tomas Mendoza watching him, a tolerant grin on his brown face. Joe nodded quickly to him.

Stepping around the lifeless body on the ground, Joe eased across the boulder and saw another man taking aim at Juan Gonzales's back. Gonzales wasn't aware that the man was there because he was expecting someone to come up from the other side.

"Hey!" Joe shouted, holding the rifle up to his shoulder. The man whirled around and Joe shot him in the chest. Gonzales's brown skin turned a little pale when he heard the shot and spun around.

Joe wanted to take Bernie Graff and especially Winston Haverty alive if possible. They were the only ones who could really tie Senator Caleb Powers to all of this. Joe also had one more reason for wanting Winston Haverty alive. Haverty had had Armando Cavazos kill Jack Lucas, a Texas Ranger.

Leaving the protection of the boulder, Joe moved up to a smaller outcropping. From there he could see the five men spreading out below. He could have picked them off one by one, but that wasn't the way he wanted to do things.

Winston Haverty had dropped back as if he wanted to let the others take all the risks. It might be easier to take him than Joe had thought.

Easing down the north side of the outcropping, Joe stood still until Haverty backed almost into his arms. Joe stepped out and pressed the rifle barrel against Haverty's back.

"Drop you gun and don't make a sound," Joe cautioned in a low voice. "I would like nothing better than to kill you right here." To give emphasis to the threat, Joe moved the rifle barrel harder against Haverty's back. "Tell Graff to get over and tell the others to stop shooting."

Before Winston Haverty had time to call Graff, a shot rang out and Joe heard an oath yelled in Spanish. Looking past Haverty and up to the first outcropping, Joe saw Tomas Mendoza grab at his chest. Then the Mexican fell over in a dead heap without saying anything else.

"Call Graff," Joe repeated in a low growl. "Call

him or so help me, I'll kill you right here." It was all Joe could do to keep from pulling the trigger.

Haverty felt the rifle barrel tighten against his back and knew from the sound in the army scout's voice that he meant what he'd said.

"Graff, come over here," Haverty called out in a tense voice. "You other men, stop shooting. Lay down your guns."

Stepping back behind the boulder, but still keeping the rifle aimed at Haverty's back, Joe watched until Bernie Graff was within sight. Then Joe moved out again. Graff had lowered the pistol to his side, but he wouldn't have needed it if looks could kill. Joe saw him move his right arm as if to bring the gun up again. Joe moved back over behind Haverty.

"Haverty," Joe said in a relatively calm voice, pushing the rifle against the short man's back again, "tell him to drop it or you're a dead man."

Joe saw Winston Haverty gripping his hands into fists and he could almost hear the wheels spinning around inside Haverty's head.

"Do what he says, Graff," Haverty said in a shaky voice. "He's probably crazy enough to do it."

Joe saw decisions made and discarded in Graff's mind. Finally reason and common sense overtook revenge, and Graff dropped his pistol.

"Now, Haverty, tell your other hired guns that they don't have any business here," Joe said, taking and expelling a deep breath. "Tell them to ride out."

"You're going to be sorry you're doing this," Haverty threatened in a cold voice. Rage was in his beady brown eyes when he looked over his shoulder at Joe.

"Not as sorry as you're going to be if you don't do what you're told," Joe shot back.

"Just who in the devil are you anyway?" Graff asked, a snarl pulling his bearded mouth to one side. His black eyes snapped as they bored into Joe.

"I'm an army scout from Fort Davis," Joe said, and enjoyed the shocked look on the big man's face. "I don't have as much authority as the Texas Ranger that Haverty had Armando Cavazos kill, but I've got enough to take you with me to the Indian camp at Elephant Mountain." He patted the rifle with his left hand and smiled craftily. "Then we're going to Fort Davis, get Colonel Eric McRaney, and go after Senator Caleb Powers."

There wasn't enough money in the world to pay for the pleasure Joe got in seeing the horrified look that passed between Winston Haverty and Bernie Graff. They both knew that, with the added implication of Senator Caleb Powers, their days of cheating the Indians were over.

The men who had ridden in with Haverty had heard what Joe had said about them riding out and didn't waste any time in doing so. They only took time to pick up their dead companions.

"Just how are you going to make us go along with you?" Haverty asked, a little cockiness coming back into his voice. "There are only three of you now and"—he grinned cunningly at Joe—"you have to drive the cattle."

Narrowing his eyes, Joe looked at Haverty for several seconds before he made a sucking sound against his teeth. "You do present a problem. But"—he paused reflectively—"there is always a solution to every problem. I could pop you on the head, and tie you across the saddle. Or I could stake you out in these rocks, drive the cattle to Elephant Mountain, then come back and get you later."

Joe looked at Winston Haverty for a second then smiled mischievously at him. "Better yet. I could leave you tied up here and let Chief Keoni or one of his men come back and get you. The chief would really like that." Joe wanted to laugh when he saw genuine fear widen Winston Haverty's eyes.

"Sanchez, which idea sounds the best to you?" Joe called out. Rique Sanchez had been standing only a few feet away listening to all of this.

"I like popping him over the head best," Sanchez said, rubbing his hands together, a gleam in his dark eyes. "I have heard that it hurts bad to be tied across a saddle." Sanchez smiled dubiously at Haverty. "Do you want me to hit him?" Sanchez took a step toward the short man, who looked even shorter as he cowered before Joe.

"You can't do that to us!" Winston Haverty wailed, a pitiful look in his pleading eyes. "Each one of those things would kill us!"

"It would be fast and a lot better than starving to death like the Indians are doing," Joe reminded him in a cold voice.

"I'll make you a deal, Howard," Winston Haverty said, a different expression racing across his face. Joe

144

had wondered how long it would take him to get around to thinking about it. Haverty's eyes looked hopeful and he took a deep breath.

"What?" Joe asked, lowering the rifle just a little although it was still aimed enough at Haverty for him to know who was in charge.

"Graff and I will help you and them"—he indicated Sanchez and Gonzales with a quick nod of his head toward the two men, who were listening with amused expressions on their brown faces—"drive those cows to the Indians if you'll let us go afterward." Haverty looked over at Graff, and Joe wasn't really surprised when the big man nodded his head quickly.

"What's to keep you from just riding away?" Joe asked skeptically.

"Something tells me that if we did that," Haverty replied, arching one brow and ducking his head to the side, "you'd come after both of us and wouldn't stop until you found us."

Joe knew that Winston Haverty and Bernie Graff were the only ones who could implicate Senator Caleb Powers in all of this and Powers was the one Joe wanted.

"I'll make you a deal," Joe said, looking Haverty straight in the eye. "I'll let you and him go," Joe said, glancing over at Graff with disgust in his voice and eyes, "after we get to Elephant Mountain if you'll write out a statement about Senator Caleb Powers's part in all of this."

Disbelief widened Haverty's eyes and his mouth gaped open. "You've got to be really crazy!" The accusation rushed out of Haverty's mouth so fast that it seemed like one long word. "Powers would kill me in a second if I did that."

"No, he won't," Joe argued, shaking his head in short jerks. "How would he know? All I need is your written statement. As soon as we leave the Indians, we'll go to Fort Davis, tell Colonel McRaney about Powers, and let him arrest him. It would do the colonel good to be able to arrest Powers."

Things were beginning to sound simple again, and therefore, they were bound to go wrong.

Winston Haverty looked down at the ground for a long time as he considered his options. His thinking took long enough for a reddish-brown centipede to crawl across his foot.

"Maybe I can make your decision easier for you," Joe said, shifting his weight from one foot to the other. Haverty's head snapped up. "Either you help me get Powers or I'll turn you both over to Chief Keoni when we get to Elephant Mountain and tell him you're the one who's been sending him all that bad meat. I'm sure that you know what Indians are capable of doing to white people."

Winston Haverty lapsed into thoughtful silence as he considered his three horrible choices.

"It's entirely your choice what happens to you and Graff," Joe said, narrowing his eyes and tilting his head to one side.

There must have been a lot of conviction in the army scout's words because Winston Haverty slowly raised his head, looked at Joe, then nodded slowly. The short man who had looked so arrogant and self-assured before was a pitiful sight now.

"Sanchez," Joe called out, "come here, pick up their guns, and search both of them." Joe knew that without any guns or knives for protection, the two men wouldn't be too eager to ride away.

Bernie Graff started to protest but the steady look in Joe's eyes dissuaded him. After Sanchez had gathered up the guns and knives and put them in a saddlebag, he and Gonzales buried Mendoza with rocks.

Joe found a note pad and pencil in Haverty's saddlebags and dictated what he wanted Haverty to write. After Joe read it to be sure that Haverty had put down on paper exactly what he wanted, Joe handed it back to Haverty to sign. When the little man had done this, Joe folded the paper, put it in his shirt pocket, and buttoned the flap.

Then the five men rode to the walled arroyo, headed the cattle out, and began the rest of the drive to the Indian camp at Elephant Mountain. Sanchez and Gonzales rode at the back and side of the herd with Joe. That way they could keep an eye on the cattle, Haverty, and Graff at the same time.

When night came, Joe knew that he wouldn't have any trouble out of Winston Haverty. But Bernie Graff presented a problem. If Joe had been in the big man's place, he would try to escape before getting to Elephant Mountain. However, Joe decided to give him the benefit of the doubt.

"Graff, if you'll give me your word that you won't try to escape," Joe said after they'd found a small stream and decided it would be a good place to spend the night, "I won't tie you up or sit here with a gun on you all night." Joe, Sanchez, and Gonzales were going to stand guard but Joe didn't want Graff to think it was going to be because of him.

"No, I won't try to escape," Graff snapped hostilely, then added with a bared-tooth snarl, "and you dang sure won't tie me up all night either."

Joe started to say something but Haverty interrupted. "I gave Howard my word that we wouldn't try to leave, Graff. There won't be any need to tie either of us up or post a guard to be sure that we stay. But I do hope that Mr. Howard will be able to keep both of us safe after we get to the Indian camp."

Joe wondered if Haverty meant keep them safe from the Indians or night predators as he poured water into the coffeepot and watched Sanchez make tortillas for supper.

Something had been gnawing at the back of Joe's brain and it wasn't until he leaned back against the trunk of an oak tree that it finally surfaced. Haverty hadn't said anything about Armando Cavazos being dead and he hadn't mentioned having Jack Lucas killed even though Joe had brought it up earlier. Joe had thought that Haverty would want to make a deal about giving him Powers if he would forget about his part in having the Texas Ranger killed.

Joe meant to keep his word and let the two men go after they got the cattle to Chief Keoni. But that didn't mean they couldn't be arrested later either by a sheriff, a U.S. marshall, or a colonel in the U.S. army. He was positive that there was no way Colonel Eric

McRaney would let them go, especially if Senator Caleb Powers was involved with them.

Joe's thoughts must have run on a telepathic track to Rique Sanchez, who was chewing on a bite of tortilla. Sanchez stood up and walked slowly over to Joe.

"Señor," he said hesitantly after swallowing, "I would not begin to tell you how to do your job since I know who you are." He paused and looked sideways at Joe. "But are you forgetting that Winston Haverty had Armando Cavazos kill that Ranger? Haverty has been in on this cattle business all along. I do not think that he should go free after we get the cattle to the Indians."

Joe took a last sip of coffee, tossed the remains out, then looked up at Sanchez shrewdly.

"Don't worry about that, Sanchez," Joe said, pulling his hat down over his face and stretching his legs out in front of him. "Those two men aren't going anywhere. I just gave Haverty *my* word that *I* would let them go. I didn't say anything about the army or a marshall. And you can bet your last dollar that Senator Powers won't go down by himself." Joe shook his head as a satisfied smile eased across his face. Sanchez looked down at Joe as a grin twinkled in his dark eyes and he seemed to relax. Joe knew that the talk he'd had with the three men at the cantina had done some good.

As Joe's eyes began closing, he had the uneasy feeling they were being watched. They weren't that far from the Indian camp and he knew that Keoni would have lookouts posted long before now.

149

A coyote, howling in the mountains, or was it a coyote, was the last thing that Joe heard before his eyes closed. He was sure that one of the Mexicans would stay wake to watch over Winston Haverty and Bernie Graff. From the hard looks they'd been throwing at the two white men, Joe knew they felt the same way about them as he did.

Joe was awakened the next morning by someone rattling the coffeepot. He opened his eyes and discovered that his neck was stiff when he tried to turn his head. He was surprised to see none other than Winston Haverty putting coffee and water in the pot over a small fire.

He's really trying to stay on my good side, Joe thought rancorously, getting slowly to his feet. Joe glanced around to see where everybody was. Bernie Graff was still asleep, stretched flat out on the ground. Juan Gonzales was leaning against an oak tree almost snoring. Just as Joe had expected, Rique Sanchez was wide awake. He and Joe exchanged meaningful looks.

After breakfast and everything had been gathered up, the five men started out on the last few miles to the Indian camp. The mountain which resembled the pachyderm for which it was named loomed in the distance. The top of the mountain looked like a huge head that curved down and sloped up like a trunk.

They had probably gone a quarter-mile when suddenly all the hairs on the back of Joe's neck stood out straight. A hard knot pulled in his stomach and his heart began pounding faster than it had since the day he was born.

150

The feelings had no more than washed over him when he looked up at the high ridge above them and saw the reason for the feelings. About ten Indians, although they didn't appear to pose a threat because there were no guns, bows, or arrows in their hands, watched the cattle and men go through a narrow canyon.

The canyon opened up into a wide, almost flat mesa. Scattered around the area were mud and twig huts. The Indians had probably known for at least a day that the men and cattle were coming because Chief Keoni was standing in front of the largest huts, a grateful expression in his dark eyes. There was just a hint of a smile on his bronze face. Joe was amazed at the regal bearing that the men presented as he stood there with his arms folded across his chest. He wore a bright red shirt, light brown pants with the legs tucked in calf-high boots, and a red band, which kept his chin-length bushy black hair from blowing in the strong afternoon breeze.

Joe and the other men dismounted, tying their horses to several juniper trees. Joe knew that it would be up to him to approach Keoni but he was surprised when the Apache began walking toward him in long easy steps.

"Joe Howard," Keoni greeted him, a solemn smile on his face, if a tiny movement of the mouth could be called a smile, "you told me you would bring good meat to my people. You told me you could ride the moon south. The good spirits of my fathers must have been with you all the way."

Joe extended his hand and was surprised when

Keoni shook it in a firm grip. A chant began on the opposite side of the village. Joe and Keoni turned simultaneously at the sound. The braves who had been up on the ridge were helping Sanchez and Gonzales drive the cattle cross the mesa to a makeshift pen.

"Did some men bring you meat earlier this week?" Joe asked, touching Keoni on the shoulder to get his attention.

"Yes," Keoni answered gravely, his mouth curling up into a tight snarl. "It was as bad as the rest."

Rage shot through Joe Howard like a hot river. "Where is the meat?" he asked, taking a deep breath to control his anger and to keep from going after Winston Haverty and beating the daylights out of him right then.

"This way," Keoni said, and started walking ahead of Joe. He led the way down a slope and into a small recess in the side of it. The sun's rays would never reach there and it was always nice and cool inside. Keoni walked over to a wagon covered with a tarpaulin that was tied down at the four corners. Even before Keoni untied the rope and pulled the tarpaulin back, Joe could smell the odor of rancid meat. He felt his stomach roll over when he pushed the cover back. He couldn't believe that anyone would give people something like this to eat! Taking a knife from his pocket, he cut off a chunk of meat and walked over into the bright sunlight. A bitter taste burned in his throat, and he swallowed hard. He knew it wouldn't take much for him to vomit.

Common sense told Joe Howard that if the Indians

had gotten the cattle on the hoof, even the skinniest cow would have given a little good meat. But the cows had been slaughtered in Marathon, and even though the meat had been salted down, the distance and the heat were just too much. There was no way it wouldn't spoil. The meat was a dull red, almost black, and it had a slick texture to it. Joe wanted to vomit again and almost did. The meat was just a shade away from being rotten.

"Is that all of the meat you got?" Joe asked, jerking his thumb over his shoulder at the small wagon. If all the hind quarters and shoulders of the cows in the third pen had been dressed out for the Indians, there would have been more meat than what was in the one wagon.

"Yes," Keoni replied with a bewildered frown.

Walking back to the wagon, Joe jerked the tarpaulin back over the meat in disgust. With the chunk of meat still in his hand, Joe and Keoni walked back to the huts.

"How do you cook this?" Joe asked, holding the putrid mess at arm's length. But even at that distance he could still smell it.

"It is boiled," Keoni answered complacently, a sad expression in his eyes as he looked up at Joe and then down at the ground.

Joe had seen an iron pot on a tripod over a fire as they rode into the village. A perverse smile twinkled in his eyes as he caught Keoni by the arm and led him toward the pot.

Bewilderment pulled a slight frown between Keoni's eyes again until Joe tossed the meat into the bubbling water and cast a scornful look at Winston Haverty and Bernie Graff, who were standing with the Mexicans at the far edge of the village.

Joe noticed a satisfied grin on Winston Haverty's small face. He was positive the little man was sure he had really put one over on Joe Howard. Haverty was probably thinking that Joe was still just a stupid army scout and had gotten one lucky break.

It didn't take the meat long to boil in the already scalding hot water. Joe didn't want to make himself appear foolish and ask for a fork. Instead he saw a long stick, which was probably intended for that purpose anyway, picked it up, and jabbed it into the now gray-colored hunk of meat.

"Haverty," Joe called out, rancor in his voice, "you and Graff, come over here." He beckoned with his right arm.

The two men hesitated for a second then started walking slowly toward him.

"I want you both to have a taste of this," Joe said, a sarcastic and compelling smile on his face. He watched Winston Haverty intently. He saw the man's lips curl instantly and his nose twitch at the awful smell. The cooking hadn't helped at all. In fact, it had made the smell worse and the steam carried the odor a good distance across the village. Even the Mexicans standing across the way put their hands over their noses.

"Go ahead," Joe insisted, holding the stick out to Haverty first. "Taste it. This is what you and Senator Caleb Powers have been sending these people to eat for the past year." Joe's eyes darkened and snapped in rage. "If you don't taste this on your own, I'm going to ram it down your throat!"

Haverty saw truth in Joe's blazing eyes and knew that the army scout would do what he said. Taking the stick slowly from Joe, Haverty pulled off a small piece and put it gingerly in his mouth. Before he could even chew once, he spit it out, turned away, and began vomiting. Bernie Graff spun around and starting to run toward the horses. Joe jerked the Colt .45 from the holster, pulled the hammer back, and aimed it at Graff.

"Hold it, Graff," Joe said in a steady but deadly voice. "You've been in on this, too. I think you should know what these people have been trying to live on."

"You'll have to shoot me before I'll eat that stuff," Graff said, a wild look in his black eyes as he spun around to face Joe.

"Don't tempt me," Joe growled, shaking his head slowly.

"But they're just—" Graff began in a whining voice.

"They're just people," Joe interrupted, aiming the pistol directly at Graff's midsection. "From this distance, I can't miss, Graff. You'd better eat it."

Knowing he had no choice, Bernie Graff walked slowly back to where Joe, Keoni, and a pale Winston Haverty were standing. Reaching out, he took a small piece of the meat, put it into his mouth, and chewed once. He got no further than that before he spit it out and ran back to the horses for his canteen.

"Tell some of your men to run that whole wagon

of rotten meat over the edge of the mesa," Joe said to Keoni, who was standing a little wide-eyed next to Joe.

In a guttural language that Joe couldn't and would probably never understand, Keoni said something and four braves ran down the slope. It wasn't long before a crash was heard as the wagon and its rotten cargo went hurtling over the edge of the bluff. A shout went up as the sound died away.

"I'm going to personally see that this never happens again," Winston Haverty said, taking a deep, shuddering breath and swallowing hard as he took a white handkerchief from his pocket and wiped his face. "Chief Keoni, you will never know how sorry I am about this. When I get back to Marathon, I'm going to notify Silas Bruell to get another herd of cattle together especially for you."

Joe didn't know which was worse: the rotten meat or Winston Haverty's simpering promise. They both made him sick to his stomach. "Oh, you're not going back to Marathon," Joe said in a smooth voice, a minute smile on his mouth. His eyes narrowed under arched brows. "You are going with us to Fort Davis," Joe reminded.

"But you told me you'd let me and Graff go if I gave you a statement about Caleb Powers," Haverty whined, a worried look beginning in his eyes.

"I did," Joe said, nodding his head slowly. "But I didn't say anything about not holding you two for the murder of Jack Lucas. He was a Texas Ranger, you know. The Indians still might want to talk to you about this meat."

Joe Howard had made the mistake of holstering the .45 as he talked to Haverty and had turned his full attention to the little man. Suddenly he felt as if he had been hit by a train when Bernie Graff came at him in a mad run. The big bearlike man would make at least one and a half of the army scout.

Joe wouldn't have shot him anyway. That would have been murder. But then Joe realized that Haverty and Graff had plotted with Armando Cavazos to kill Jack Lucas.

Graff bent over, grabbed Joe around the knees, and they both hit the ground. All the air was knocked out of Joe as Graff fell on top of him. Joe managed to pull in a short breath as Graff rolled away. Joe thought that he would be more agile than Graff because he was smaller. But that wasn't to be the case. Joe scrambled to his feet but Graff was up as soon as Joe was and lunged at him again. Joe was amazed at the big man's agility.

If Bernie Graff happened to get lucky and hit Joe with one of his hamlike fists, it would take Joe's head from his shoulders. Joe had been in fistfights before but never with a man this big. Joe sidestepped as Graff rushed past him. But with the grace of a cat, Graff spun back around and grinned at Joe. Deep in his black eyes was a threat.

"You're not going to leave me here with these dirty, stinking Indians," Graff bellowed. With the fury of a madman glistening in his eyes, Graff started at Joe again, his huge arms reaching out.

Joe Howard had no choice. He would regret this next action, but not right now. Jerking the Colt .45

157

from the holster, he aimed it at Graff and hoped that he would stop when he saw it. But Graff kept coming.

"Stop, Graff," Joe called out to the big man, who was bent low now and still advancing toward him. "Don't do it. Don't make me kill you."

But a lot of hate and maybe a little self-preservation kept pushing Graff. Joe pulled the trigger. The blast caught Graff in the chest. Graff clutched at the front of his shirt. His big legs began shaking. His knees buckled and he seemed to go down in slow motion. Bernie Graff, who disliked someone laughing at his name, was dead before he hit the ground.

"Howard, you'll pay for this," Winston Haverty promised through clenched teeth.

"But not before you do," Joe said, contempt in his voice and eyes. He holstered the Colt .45 then took and expelled a deep breath.

"Can we throw bad man over cliff with bad meat?" Keoni asked, coming up behind Joe with soundless steps. Joe couldn't tell if the Indian was joking or serious.

"No," Joe answered, shaking his head, feeling a pull at his mouth. "He'll have to be buried. After we do that, we four,"—he nodded toward Haverty, Sanchez, and Gonzales—"are going to head to Alpine and find Senator Caleb Powers. You're welcome to go along."

Winston Haverty's face turned pale and he stared at Joe Howard.

"I will go with you," Keoni said, his voice

surprising Joe. "But you must stay here tonight. We have good meat to eat. You must eat, too. We go at first light."

Joe wasn't about to waste his time and breath arguing with the Indian. He must have a reason for wanting to wait.

Chapter 6

Joe Howard, Rique Sanchez, and Juan Gonzales buried Bernie Graff a good distance from Chief Keoni's village. The Indians would have no part in it. They would just as soon have thrown the big man's body over the bluff.

"You killed him," Winston Haverty said stubbornly, shaking his head when Joe looked around at him. "You can bury him."

"Keoni, while we're busy," Joe said, a stillness in his features, "be sure and keep an eye on that man. If he so much as moves a whisker to escape, I want you to shoot him."

Chief Keoni turned his head slowly away from Joe to look at Winston Haverty. The small man seemed to shrink even more under the Apache's intense scrutiny.

It took all three men to pick up Graff's big body and get it on the horse. Getting it down was no problem. Juan Gonzales just caught hold of the belt around the thick waist and gave it a tug. As they piled rocks around the body, Joe wondered what had been done about Armando Cavazos's body. Had Winston Haverty buried it or was it still lying out there by the cattle pens as a banquet for the buzzards?

The sun began setting behind the mountains, which were a brilliant red in the slow descending rays. A warm breeze that would turn cold after the sun went down swept across the village. The people were quiet. Most of them, especially the children, were sleeping. A cow was slaughtered and, with a speed that amazed Joe, was dressed out, a lot of it boiled, and most of that eaten.

Joe felt good all the way down to his toes, knowing that one wrong had been righted against these people who only asked to be left alone to live life the way they had for years.

Joe still had jerky in his saddlebags, and not wanting to deprive the Indians of even a tiny morsel of food, he took only a small piece of the boiled meat. It wasn't bad at all. It would have tasted better in a stew or fried as a steak, but when beggars couldn't be choosers, it tasted pretty good.

Sanchez and Gonzales, probably feeling as Joe did, finished up their tortillas and pulque. Haverty wouldn't have eaten any of the meat if Joe had held a gun to his head. He made do with some jerky from his own saddlebag.

"My people have not eaten this way in long time," Chief Keoni said, gratitude in his black eyes as he looked straight at Joe. "What will Colonel McRaney do to that man?" He nodded toward Winston

Haverty, who was sitting close to Sanchez and Gonzales.

"He will probably make him a deal not to press any charges if he'll turn evidence against Senator Powers," Joe said, shrugging his shoulders. "But he just can't let him go free," Joe continued, stretching his legs out in front of him. "He and Graff had a man killed who was a Texas Ranger."

Night settled over the village and brought the sounds of birds and coyotes, and the water could be heard on the Calamity River not far away. A fire had been rebuilt in the circle of rocks. Joe could see Haverty and the two Mexicans still sitting on the opposite side of the village. He wondered what Haverty had in mind when the little man stood up. Maybe he was going to answer nature's call. But he was surprised when Haverty walked up and stood in front of him.

"If we're going to spend the night here," Haverty said, "I don't want to sleep outside. I want to sleep in one of those small huts. I'll feel safer in there. Make someone give me theirs."

It took all of Joe's willpower not to laugh at the pompous little man standing there with such arrogance, demanding what he did and didn't want.

"You'll be a lot safer out here," Joe said, easing his eyes slowly up to meet Haverty's, "where I can keep an eye on you. If you're alone, someone could slip in and cut your throat." He made a cutting motion across his own throat. He enjoyed it when Haverty turned pale. "These people don't like you very much, you know."

Joe saw real fear widen Haverty's brown eyes in the flickering light and he shook his head mentally when Haverty sat down beside him on the ground. Haverty was so close to Joe that he could feel the heat from the little man's shoulders. The desire to ride away and leave this man alone with the Indians was strong in Joe Howard. The Indians wouldn't kill him but the scare probably would.

Joe went to sleep where he sat, not even bothering to get up for his bedroll. He awoke once during the night. The Indians had gone into their huts, but Winston Haverty was as close as he could get to Joe without actually touching him.

I should shoot this low-down snake right here, Joe thought, cold dislike pulling a hard knot in his stomach and a bitter taste in his mouth. He was such a big man as long as he had his cronies around and was cheating people out of food.

But he knew that he had to keep Winston Haverty alive. He would need him to implicate Senator Caleb Powers in all of this. Joe cursed himself for not taking the paper from the folder in Haverty's desk with Powers's name on it.

Even though Winston Haverty had signed the paper and Joe had it in his pocket implicating Powers, Haverty could say that Joe had forced him to sign it, and in a way, he would be right. It was either sign the paper or get tied up and left alone in the mountains or let the Indians come back and get him. Joe knew that if he had been in Haverty's once-shiny boots, he would have signed the papers in nothing flat.

If something happened to Winston Haverty before they reached Fort Davis, it would only be Joe's word against Senator Caleb Powers, and Joe knew that without some definite proof, Powers could get away free as a bird. Joe didn't think that Sanchez and Gonzales would talk unless they knew it would save their necks. But there was nothing he could actually do to make them go along with him.

Maybe he should go back to Marathon and get the paper with Powers's name on it. He should have already done that. With the assurance in his mind now that nothing would go wrong, Joe went back to sleep.

Joe was awakened by Chief Keoni shaking him on the shoulder as the gray half-light of dawn announced the beginning of a new day.

Alpine was a two-day ride from Elephant Mountain and a one-day ride to Fort Davis. Joe decided, along with Chief Keoni, Sanchez, and Gonzales, not to go straight to Alpine. Instead he thought that it would be a better idea to avoid Alpine and Senator Caleb Powers right then and go on to Fort Davis instead. They could use Colonel Eric McRaney's help.

Joe knew that Winston Haverty wouldn't accept all the blame for the bad meat the Indians had been getting. No sane man would do that. No matter what else Haverty might be, he certainly wasn't insane.

Joe also knew that Colonel Eric McRaney didn't like Powers and would really enjoy taking him into custody. Joe didn't have the authority to arrest anyone anyway, but was hoping that Haverty would think that he did and wouldn't give him any kind of trouble.

The presence of Chief Keoni had put an entirely different attitude into Winston Haverty. Joe noticed that Haverty didn't ride too far away from him. In fact, he kept his horse only a few feet from Joe's right side. The short man kept glancing over his shoulder at the Apache leader, who rode behind and a little to the left of Joe. Keoni seemed to have his black eyes glued on Haverty. Sanchez and Gonzales rode behind and to the right of Haverty.

They rode about two miles from Keoni's village when Joe held up his hand for them to stop. Winston Haverty's face turned as white as snow when Joe told them that he was going back to Marathon.

"Chief Keoni," Joe said, reining Serge around to face the Indian, "Colonel McRaney knows you. He will believe you when you tell him what has happened. It will probably take you two days to get to Fort Davis. I need a paper that is in Haverty's desk. Whatever you do, don't let that man get away." He nodded toward Winston Haverty, who was almost trembling in the saddle.

"Howard, don't leave me alone with him," Haverty screamed, his eyes wide in fear. "He'll kill me. Please, take me with you. I'll see to it that you get everything you need to use against Powers. That Indian will kill me for sure."

"He won't if you don't try to get away," Joe promised sarcastically, pulling his mouth into a tight grin. He enjoyed the distress on Haverty's face. He liked hearing the little man beg.

166

"Chief," Joe said mildly, "I do want to see this man alive when I get to Fort Davis." The Indian's black eyes didn't change their expression. They probably wouldn't have changed if he picked his foot up from hot coals and put it down on a chunk of ice.

The two men of different races looked at each other for a long time. A slight threat was in the brown eyes. A steadiness was in the black eyes. Joe knew that they were wasting time with this cat-and-mouse game. Without saying anything, he reined Serge around and set off at a steady gallop back to Marathon.

Since he didn't have the cattle to slow him down, it took a lot less time to reach Marathon than he'd expected. It was almost noon when he saw the office and the now empty cattle pens and started in that direction.

But suddenly the craving for a good cup of coffee assaulted his taste buds and he knew that the best place in town for coffee was at the hotel. With a grin on his face, which sported a two-week growth of beard, he admitted that coffee was as good an excuse as any to see Saber Entonelli.

Pulling Serge to a stop in front of the hotel, he dismounted, tied the reins, and went inside. As before, she was sitting behind the counter with a newspaper spread out before her. Her long black hair hung down her back in one thick curl. An orange blouse tucked down into an orange, blue, and green skirt accentuated the olive hue of her skin. The outline of her breasts was visible at the top of the blouse.

"How about a cup of coffee?" Joe asked, walking

167

lightly up to her. She was so lost in what she was reading that she almost jumped out of her skin at the sound of his voice.

"What in the world are you doing here?" Saber asked, crumpling the edge of the paper in her hand. The color drained from her face and her mouth gaped open. "There's a warrant out for your arrest."

Joe stared at her for a minute across the desk. If her long-lashed black eyes hadn't been wide in surprise, he would have thought that she was trying to play a joke on him. But there was no joking in the frown pulling between her dark eyes.

"Arrest?" Joe repeated, feeling his mouth go dry. "For what?" He'd spent just one night in Marathon and the only trouble he'd gotten into while in town was when he and Bernie Graff had mixed it up over Graff's first name in the livery. He didn't think that that was cause enough for a man to get arrested.

Joe's heart suddenly started pounding against his ribs when he remembered killing Armando Cavazos in Brewster. But he had explained all of that to Sheriff Pierce Jagger. Explained that it had been in self-defense. And he had also explained that Cavazos had killed Jack Lucas, who was a Texas Ranger. He also remembered that Sheriff Jagger hadn't seemed too interested in any of it at the time.

Suddenly everything fell into place when he reminded himself that Sheriff Jagger was working with Winston Haverty. Haverty must have told Jagger a different story when he arrived in Brewster to get his cattle and found Cavazos's body. To stay on Haverty's good side, if the man really had a good side,

168

Sheriff Jagger had put out the arrest warrant.

"What kind of law is here in Marathon?" Joe asked, licking his dry mouth and taking a deep breath. All he needed was just enough time to get to Haverty's desk at the cattle pens, find the folder with the paper which would implicate Senator Caleb Powers, and get out of town.

"It might surprise you to know that we have a U.S. marshall," Saber answered, a sorrowful expression in her eyes. "He had to go up to Fort Stockton for a hearing but should be back any day. In fact, he should have already been back. If you hurry, you should have time to do whatever you came to do." Urgency was in her eyes and voice.

"I've got to get a paper from Winston Haverty's office," Joe said, jerking his thumb over his shoulder toward Haverty's office up the street.

"Do you know where Haverty is?" Saber asked, dropping the paper and folding her hands on top of it.

"Yeah," Joe answered, a mirthless grin pulling at the corners of his mouth. "He's on his way to Fort Davis with an Apache Indian and two Mexicans." He wondered how the four men were getting along. He wished he could have been a bird in the sky watching.

Saber Entonelli threw back her head and her bell-sounding laughter filled the room. Slapping her hands down on the countertop, she leaned over them, still laughing.

"Did you just say that Winston Haverty is going to Fort Davis with an Apache Indian and two Mexicans?" she asked, rising up and taking a long breath when her amused laughter finally ended. She wrinkled up her forehead, still trying without much success to compose herself.

"Yeah," Joe answered, and grinned when she closed her eyes and shook her head.

"I'd pay to see that," she said, standing up and reaching under the counter. "I wish the pompous little twit would try something and the Indian would kill him." Taking out a paper sack, she handed it to Joe. "These are your clothes. You left before Mrs. Onrota finished with them. Do you still want that cup of coffee?"

Even though he was in a hurry, Joe knew that a few minutes spent with Saber wouldn't make that much difference. "Sure," he said, and followed her into her own quarters.

The coffeepot was on the back of the stove and it didn't take long for Saber to stoke up the fire and make a fresh pot of coffee. The enticing aroma soon filled the room and tasted good with a slice of apple pie.

"What do you think will happen to Haverty?" Saber asked, curling her hands around a cup of coffee and peering at Joe over the rim as she took a tiny sip.

"I don't know," Joe answered, after swallowing a bite of pie, "if being with the Indian doesn't scare him to death. He won't try to escape because he's unarmed. All I want him to do is testify against Senator Caleb Powers. And that really is a government affair." Pushing the plate back, he drained the coffee cup and stood up.

"Are you going right now?" she asked, putting her

cup down and standing up. Joe saw a wistfulness in her eyes.

"Yeah," he answered, noticing a different feeling in his knees as he looked down at her upturned face. "I want to hurry and find that paper and get to Fort Davis to be sure that Winston Haverty is there. I have a signed confession by him but he could say that he only did it under pressure."

Saber walked around the table and flicked some imaginary particle from his shirtsleeve. "What are you going to do when all of this is over?" Her voice dropped a little and her eyes deepened with something way in the back of them.

"I'd thought about going fishing," Joe answered slowly, his heart taking off again in rapid beating, but for another reason this time. The look in her eyes promised something a lot better than fishing.

"There's a river not too far from here," she said, arching her brows and holding his gaze. "You could probably catch something to your liking."

Joe Howard would have been a first-class fool if he hadn't taken advantage of his present opportunity. He had never been called a fool before.

"You're probably right," he said, sliding one arm around her waist and the other around her shoulders and bringing her up tightly against him. This time they were both ready for the kiss. There was no gratitude in it as there had been when Joe had told her about his reason for being in Marathon. This was just a kiss between a man and a woman. Her mouth was warm and open when he lowered his head, and he could feel her tongue playing games with his. She wound her arms tightly around his neck.

The little voice in the back of his mind finally made itself heard over the roaring in his ears, telling him that he had other things to do. Not necessarily more important things to do, but nevertheless, other things. Hugging her tightly against him, Joe took a deep breath, lifted his head, and stepped back.

"You know," he said, smiling roguishly down at her, while drawing his finger down the side of her flushed cheek, "you just might be right. After all of this is over, don't be surprised to see me again. Keep the coffeepot hot."

Bending down, he put another quick kiss on her parted and smiling mouth, pulled his hat down, picked up the clothes sack, and walked to the door. "What do you fish with?" he asked, tilting his head to one side and looking at her.

"Anything it takes," she answered, a steady but meaningful expression in her dark eyes. Joe grinned when she touched her lips with the tip of her tongue.

"I'll be back," he said, expelling a deep breath and going outside.

Something told him not to take Serge to the cattle pens and he would be glad later that he heeded that advice. Taking only enough time to stick the clothes sack in the saddlebags, Joe hurried down the street and opened the door to Haverty's office. Rushing over to the desk, he sat down as he had before, opened the drawer, and saw the yellow folder below some plain white paper. Opening the folder, he removed the sheet of paper that had not only Senator Caleb Powers's name on it, but Winston Haverty's name and dates and amounts of cattle that Powers had gotten on it. Folding the paper, he put it into his shirt pocket along with the one that Haverty had already signed.

He had just put the folder back in the drawer and closed it when he heard footsteps outside the window. Frantically, he looked around the room for someplace to hide. But he didn't see anything and there was no darkness to protect him as there had been the last time. The sun was shining brightly outside. He had just started to crawl under the desk when he heard Saber's voice outside.

"Well, hello, Marshall Russak," she said in a loud voice to be sure that Joe would hear her. "What brings you over here? I thought you were still in Fort Stockton."

"I could ask you the same thing," the man's gruff voice replied. Joe could tell that he was just outside the door now. "I thought I saw a man go in here."

"Who would have the nerve to go into Winston Haverty's office when he's gone?" she asked keenly. From the sound of her voice, Joe could tell that she was coming closer to the man standing at the door. "You know what kind of man he is. Mean as a hungry wolf. Your tired eyes could just be playing tricks on you. Come on over to the hotel and I'll make you a good cup of coffee."

Joe wondered if her invitation would go any further. He got his answer when she called out "Just coffee" in a loud voice. He grinned. But then he frowned. He didn't know if her last two words were for his benefit or were a rebuff to Russak.

"You've got a deal," Russak said. "I guess my eyes are tired. Do you know who owns that black horse in front of the hotel?" Russak continued. The boards in front of the door squeaked and Joe knew that he was moving away.

"Yeah," Saber answered, her voice getting fainter. "He's just a saddle bum who rode in a few minutes ago wanting a room. He was so drunk that he left the horse's reins untied."

"I'm going to love that woman for the rest of my life," Joe said in a low voice as he stood up from behind the desk. Standing still for a moment, he took a long breath and adjusted the gunbelt around his waist. Opening the door a crack, he was just in time to see Saber and a tall, thin man going into the hotel. She paused long enough to hold out her left hand with the fingers crossed.

Joe opened the door, stepped out, put his finger and thumb to his mouth, and whistled for Serge. It only took the black horse a few seconds to come the distance. Joe swung up into the saddle, slammed his heels into Serge's side, and they rode out of Marathon in a cloud of dust.

Joe felt that he was far enough away from Marathon to avoid arrest when he stopped for the night. The sun still had about two hours to shine but he was tired and decided that was enough for the day. He would have liked nothing better than to ride by Alpine and see if Senator Caleb Powers was there or if Winston Haverty's disclosure to Eric McRaney had infuriated the colonel so much that he'd already gone after him.

Joe hoped not. He wanted to be along when the "pompous ass" was made to pay for his part in all of this. He was glad that Chief Keoni was along.

The wind was warm. Joe kicked out the bedroll and stretched out on the top blanket. He had unsaddled Serge and was using the saddle as a pillow. The desert sounds had almost lulled him off to sleep when they were interrupted by the distant clatter of steady-paced hoofs. He had wanted to sit there and rest and think about Saber Entonelli.

Jumping up, he hurried over to Serge, who was tied under a cottonwood tree and as a precaution clamped his hand tightly over his nose. He didn't know if the rider would be someone following him or someone just riding through. But that was a stupid thought. Whoever it was had to be following him. As vast as the area was, how could someone just happen to come the exact way he had?

The horse began slowing down and an amused grin eased across Joe's face. It was none other than Marshall Russak. Apparently the lawman hadn't believed all that Saber Entonelli had told him. Joe had thought he'd put enough distance between him and Marathon that nobody would catch up with him this soon.

He saw Russak ease back on the reins and the horse slowed even more. He was almost to a walk. Russak bent his tall body almost double as he leaned over to look down at the ground. Joe hadn't made any effort to hide his tracks but he didn't think that he'd be this easy to follow in such rocky terrain.

Joe knew that he hadn't done anything illegal in

Marathon. He had killed Armando Cavazos in Brewster and that was well out of Russak's jurisdiction. No wait a minute! Joe thought, shaking his head with a quick jerk. A U.S. marshall had jurisdiction over everything and could go anywhere. Russak could even follow Joe right up to the front door of Eric McRaney's office at Fort Davis if he wanted to. But would he be able to arrest him there?

But maybe the marhsall's presence could be an aid to Joe. He wasn't sure who would have jurisdiction over a senator but it wouldn't hurt to have him along.

Removing his hand from Serge's nose, Joe pulled his Colt .45 from its holster and stepped out from behind the tree.

"Drop your gun and get down," Joe called out. He saw the tall man stiffen in the saddle a second before he used his left hand to take a pistol from the holster on his left side and drop it to the ground. "Now, the rifle," Joe continued, walking over to squat down and pick up the pistol while still keeping an eye on the man lowering a Henry rifle to the ground. Pushing the pistol down in his belt, Joe picked up the rifle then straightened up. He stepped back, well out of the tall man's reach, never taking his eyes off of him.

"I'm probably the man you're looking for," Joe said in a steady voice. "I'm Joe Howard, an army scout out of Fort Davis. You're probably after me for killing a man in Brewster. I'm sure that if you hadn't heard a different story from Sheriff Pierce Jagger on what had actually happened, you wouldn't be here."

The tall man swung down with what seemed to be

no effort at all.

"If you're the one who killed Armando Cavazos," the man said in a lazy drawl, "you are the one I'm looking for. I'm Marshall Carl Russak." He tapped the five-pronged tin badge pinned to a gray shirt. There was annoyance in the deep-set green eyes.

Joe could tell from the arrogant way that Russak stood and spoke that it was going to take a lot of talking to convince him that he was on the right side of the law.

"How did you know that I was the one who had killed Cavazos in the first place?" Joe asked, keeping the pistol aimed at the tall, thin man. Something didn't make sense here.

"It's simple," Russak answered glibly, pushing a wide-brimmed tan hat back on his close-cropped hair. "Sheriff Jagger in Brewster sent me a wire. You made the mistake of telling him that you'd killed the Mexican because he'd seen you shoot a Texas Ranger."

The tall marshall's words hit Joe Howard right in the middle of his stomach and a thousand little black dots began swirling before his eyes. He began breathing hard. He couldn't believe what his ears were hearing.

"What?" Joe finally asked, frowning deeply at Russak. "I'll admit that I killed Armando Cavazos. But I'll swear on Bibles stacked as high as your armpit that I did not kill Jack Lucas!" He drew the last words out slowly to be sure that Russak understood them. He could hardly wait until he got to Fort Davis and could confront Winston Haverty with all of this!

Anger and disbelief tied a knot in Joe's stomach. He'd made a big mistake by telling Sheriff Jagger who he was and that he'd killed Cavazos. After Haverty found Cavazos's body, it didn't take him long to concoct a story for Jagger to tell Russak, accusing Joe of murder.

"Jack Lucas was a Texas Ranger," Joe went on taking a deep breath. The pistol wavered a little in his hand. "Lucas didn't know what was going on between Winston Haverty and Senator Caleb Powers with the cattle that the Indians were supposed to be getting. He was checking also on some rustled cattle. Jagger had recognized Lucas on the last trip to Brewster as being a Texas Ranger and had told Haverty about it."

Joe had been correct in his assumption that Russak wouldn't believe anything he'd tell him without a little persuasion.

"Marshall, if I was the killer you think I am," Joe said pragmatically, "I could have blown you right out of the saddle when I saw you coming. Killing a marshall is no different from killing a Texas Ranger. They wouldn't hang me any higher."

That point seemed to make an impression on Marshall Carl Russak. He made a sucking sound against his teeth. His green eyes narrowed as he seemed to consider what Joe had told him.

"I guess, when you put it like that," Russak said, hooking his thumbs over his pockets, "it does make some sense. What do you suggest we do now?"

Joe noticed a strange look in Russak's green eyes,

as though some kind of plot was forming in his mind. Knowing that Russak only believed about half of what he'd said, Joe would have to stay on his guard until they reached Fort Davis.

"I suggest we bed down for the night," Joe answered, uncertainty edging his voice, "then get up early tomorrow and head to Fort Davis."

Russak turned around to his horse and took up the reins. "Do I get my guns back?" he asked, looking at Joe over his shoulder. "There are probably those out here in this country who aren't as friendly as you." There was speculation in his gruff voice.

"Yeah, I guess so," Joe answered, holding out the pistol and rifle. "A man would be at a disadvantage and feel a little naked out here without some kind of protection. But," he went on, giving Russak an intense look, "I want you to know that if anything should happen to me and I don't show up at the fort in a couple of days, Colonel Eric McRaney will come looking for me. He only gave me three weeks to find out why the Indians at Elephant Mountain aren't getting the beef they'd been promised and if Senator Caleb Powers is involved in any of it."

What Joe Howard had told the marshall was only a half-lie. He knew he couldn't stay awake all night and hoped that if he dropped a powerful enough name, Russak would think twice about doing anything to him. The only thing he hoped Russak would do was leave. But there was a stubbornness about the lawman that told Joe he would stay.

"Did you say Senator Caleb Powers?" Russak asked, jerking around to look at Joe. He had unsaddled his horse and froze where he stood, staring at Joe, a deep and puzzled frown on his thin face. "Senator Caleb Powers?"

"That's the one," Joe answered lightly, taking the coffeepot, canteen, and coffee from the grub sack. "Do you know him?" He walked away and began gathering enough twigs and leaves to build a small fire to make coffee.

"I've known Caleb Powers for a long time," Russak said, taking two tin cups from his saddlebags. "He never struck me as being the type who would do anything dishonest. But I guess everybody has a price."

It didn't take long to make the coffee. It smelled and tasted good. The night had cooled off enough for the coffee not to be too hot. Russak opened his bedroll, sat down, leaned back against a tree, and stretched his long legs out in front of him.

"Since you don't really trust me," Russak said reflectively, swishing a mouthful of coffee around and through his teeth before swallowing it, "and this coffee is supposed to help keep you awake, why don't you tell me what all of this is about. You can take my word, for what it's worth to you, if the coffee doesn't work, you'll be as alive in the morning as you are right now."

Russak crossed his legs at the ankles and took another sip of coffee. Before Joe could help it, relaxed laughter erupted from his lungs and relieved a lot of tension.

Joe didn't know if it was his imagination or if Russak was as spellbound as he appeared to be as Joe told him, in minute detail, why he was here and most of the names involved. Every now and then Russak would arch his brows in surprise.

"Weren't you even suspicious or curious about what went on at the cattle pens?" Joe asked, a little accusation in his voice, refilling his cup for the third time. "It would seem to me that a U.S. marshall would know what was going on right under his nose." A sly look narrowed his brown eyes.

"No," Russak answered, shaking his head and throwing out the remains of the cold coffee in his cup. "I just thought that Winston Haverty had three buyers for Silas Bruell's cattle. I had no idea, or any reason to know, that Caleb Powers was involved in this. Are you sure?"

Joe stirred up the fire for more light, took the pieces of paper from his shirt pocket, and handed them across to Russak. The marshall took the papers, leaned closer to the fire, but still had to squint to see the incriminating names, dates, and figures on the papers.

"If I wasn't seeing this with my own eyes," Russak said, folding the papers and handing them back to Joe, "I wouldn't believe it. Caleb Powers. A U.S. senator, of all people."

Joe, believing that the surprised look on Russak's face was real, took the papers, put them back into his pocket, and buttoned the flap. He blinked his eyes several times but even the third cup of coffee wasn't much help. His eyelids became too heavy to keep open. He never knew it when his head fell back against the saddle and he dropped off to sleep.

The next thing he knew, a small band of pink was separating the earth from the sky and the aroma of coffee and frying meat filled the air. He sat up stiffly, pushed his hair back out of his face, and put his hat on.

"If we leave as soon as we've eaten," Russak said, raking half the meat into a tin plate and filling Joe's cup, "we could be at Alpine late tonight. If everything is true about Senator Powers, and I believe it is since reading those papers, we can get this whole thing cleared up in just a little while. Oh, by the way," Russak went on after putting a piece of crisp meat into his mouth and chewing, "how did you sleep last night?"

A joking grin twinkled in his green eyes as he swallowed the meat and looked at Joe over the rim of his cup. Joe could feel his face turning red because he knew what the marshall was thinking. But he wasn't going to let Russak's kidding get to him.

"Pretty good," Joe answered, downing the cup of coffee in a couple of swallows. It wasn't as strong as he really liked it but it would do. "Since I knew you wouldn't let anything happen to me, I really didn't have much to worry about. But," he went on, standing up and rolling his blankets together, "we can't go to Alpine right now. We have to go to Fort Davis first."

Joe turned around from putting the blanket and saddle on Serge when he heard Russak expel a disgruntled breath. He saw an argument building up in Russak's green eyes and a frown pulling between his thin brows.

"I'm not going to wrangle with you over this," Joe said calmly and shaking his head. A hard knot worked in his jaw. "I know that you outrank me as far as authority goes, but Colonel Eric McRaney has waited for a long time for a chance to get this man. The colonel doesn't know how deeply Powers is involved in this. McRaney has tried hard over the past year to get Powers to help the Indians more. For some reason, and we know why now, that help has been slow in coming. McRaney is going to be the one to arrest him."

The determined set of the army scout's jaw and the cold look in his brown eyes told the marshall that it would do no good for him to pursue the matter any further if he wanted to go along. If he objected too strongly, the army scout might really take matters into his own hands.

"All right," Russak agreed with a tight tone of voice, shrugging his shoulders. "You apparently know more about what's going on than I do, so we'll do it your way and see what happens."

Joe was pleased and surprised, both in equal amounts, that Russak hadn't insisted on going straight to Alpine and arresting Powers. He didn't know what he would have done if the marshall had insisted on it. Of course, they still had a long distance to cover yet and anything could happen before they reached Fort Davis.

The two days it took to reach Fort Davis passed by quicker than Joe had anticipated. In the back of his mind, he kept wondering if Chief Keoni had been able to get Winston Haverty to Fort Davis alive. He wondered if Winston Haverty had tried to make a deal with the Indian to get away and he also wondered if Rique Sanchez and Juan Gonzales had ridden all the way to the fort with Keoni and Haverty. There really was no need for them to do it. They had only been hired to do a job and that job was over. Maybe they would be curious as to the outcome of the whole thing and stick around until Joe arrived. Then he knew they would be there because he'd said he would pay them.

Russak had done nothing to get Joe to change his mind and go to Alpine first. In fact, nothing else had been said about the matter since Joe had more or less laid down the rules on how things would be.

"You know something," Joe said thoughtfully, looking at Russak as they rode along, "I never thought I'd live to see the day when three races of people would be involved in one situation."

"Well, I don't know about you," Russak said, pushing his hat back on his head, "but I feel sorry for the Indians. I couldn't say that to just anybody because I'd be called an Indian lover. You must have at least one sympathetic heartbeat, or you wouldn't be on this job. Nobody in his right mind would stand for broken promises and being pushed back very long." He looked sideways at Joe and his green eyes snapped. "I know I wouldn't."

Joe Howard was astonished to hear these words coming from a white man. It was in complete contrast to Joe's previous concept of the man. He wondered what would happen if Russak got into a conversation with Titus Upshaw at the general store in Fort Davis.

"I believe that every man who God was good enough to put on this earth should be able to live the way he chooses, as long as it doesn't hurt anyone else," Joe said, removing his hat and wiping the sweat band with a blue handkerchief. "It's morally wrong when one race of people has to suffer to benefit others."

Joe looked straight ahead at the looming granite mountains. The jagged edges seemed to scratch the blue sky. A few trees appeared to be clinging to the sides of the mountain. Behind those mountains was Fort Davis and soon he would know the outcome of what one member of the human race had done to another.

The dinner bell was being rung as Joe and Russak rode through the arched rock gate at the fort. There was no sign of the Indian horse and Joe guessed that it would be in the corral with the others. Not sure if McRaney would be eating in the mess hall or in his office, Joe led the way to the office first.

He and Russak dismounted, tied their horses to the hitch rail in front, and walked up the steps. Joe knocked on the door and expelled a relieved breath when he heard Colonel Eric McRaney's booming voice call out. His worries were over. McRaney could handle everything from here on. Joe would rest a few days if he could hide from McRaney, then ride back to Marathon and go fishing.

Things were beginning to sound simple again. But Joe got a shock when he opened the door and walked in. Eric McRaney was sitting behind his desk as usual, looking neat and clean. But leaning against the wall behind the colonel's swivel chair was the pair of wooden crutches. Joe's heart sank down to the bottom of his feet. He knew he wasn't going to like anything that McRaney would tell him. And he also knew that his fishing trip would have to be postponed.

"What in the devil happened to you?" Joe asked, spacing the words out slowly, knowing that his mouth was gaping open. He moved his gaze from McRaney, over to the crutches, and back to McRaney again. He could see all his plans going up in smoke.

"I was trying to ride one of the new horses," McRaney said, a sheepish look on his long tanned face. "He was a little more than I had bargained for and he threw me."

Maybe he'd just sprained his leg, Joe prayed silently. But that was too good to be true. Joe's heart sank when he walked around the desk and McRaney pushed the swivel chair back. McRaney's right pant leg had been cut up the side and his leg was in a splint all the way up to the knee. It was wrapped in bandages and only his toes were visible.

"How bad is it?" Joe asked, a sick feeling in the pit of his stomach.

"It's broken," McRaney replied simply, pursing his mouth and arching his brows as he looked up at Joe.

"Well," Joe said, dropping down on the edge of the desk, smiling halfheartedly and expelling a deep breath, "I've got something right here in my shirt pocket that will make you feel a little better."

An amused frown pulled between McRaney's thin black brows. "What are you talking about? Did you find out about the cattle that were supposed to be going Chief Keoni? Who is that with you?"

Joe had been so surprised by McRaney's condition that he'd completely forgotten that Marshall Carl Russak was still standing there.

Joe introduced the marshall and enjoyed the wide-eyed, expectant look in Colonel McRaney's eyes.

"Didn't Chief Keoni or Winston Haverty tell you anything when they got here?" Joe asked irritably. He had thought that the little yellow-haired man would blab his head off when he got to the fort and try to make some kind of deal with McRaney.

"No," McRaney answered, shaking his head rapidly. "Haverty started to say something one time. But Chief Keoni gave him a look that would knock a bird from a tree and said that you would be here in a few days and straighten out the whole thing."

"Marshall Russak knows Senator Powers," Joe said, a shrewd grin on his mouth.

"So?" McRaney prompted, grimacing when he hit his leg against the edge of the desk.

"So," Joe mimicked, taking the paper from his pocket. "Senator Caleb Powers has been getting the pick of the cattle that should have been going to the Indians. Haverty has been selling the next best cows to some place in Chicago, and Keoni was getting the rest."

McRaney stared up at Joe for a second. Then he began laughing. "Senator Caleb Powers is finally going to get his," he said, taking a deep breath and rubbing his hands together. His eyes narrowed, he pressed his mouth into a tight line and shook his head slowly.

"I knew you'd get a charge out of that," Joe said, reaching out and patting the colonel on the shoulder. "Not only do we have Powers's name on that paper, but we also have Winston Haverty's word and a signed statement by Haverty against Powers. Now," Joe said, slapping his hands down against his legs and standing up, "all you have to do is lead us to Alpine and arrest him."

Joe Howard was so pleased with himself. He had done what Colonel McRaney had sent him to do. The Indians would be getting good meat from now on. Winston Haverty would testify against Senator Caleb Powers, Powers would go to jail, and Joe could go fishing. Once again, everything was sounding simple.

"Well," McRaney drew out, squinting up his eyes as he looked at Joe. "There's a little problem."

"Problem?" Joe snapped. "What do you mean, problem? You said that Keoni and Haverty got here. How about two Mexicans?"

"Oh, they're here, all right," McRaney said, dropping his gaze down to his splinted leg. "But I can't go to Alpine. I can't even get on a horse. You're going to have to go to Alpine and get Powers."

"Me!" Joe said incredulously, staring down at McRaney. His brown eyes were wide in disbelief. "I don't have the authority to do that! I've already done what you told me to do. And I almost got myself killed doing that, I might add. You could ride in a wagon."

Once again McRaney laughed up at Joe. "That makes about as much sense as sending a chicken with a broken wing after a fox. A ride like that would really mess up this leg. I'll give you authority to go to Alpine. Besides, you'll have a U.S. marshall with you."

Joe looked down at Colonel Eric McRaney and wondered for the hundredth time why things seemed so simple when he explained them and then always turned out to be a disaster.

"To make things really legal," Marshall Carl Russak said, a wide grin on his up-until-now stoic face, "I'll swear you in as a deputy U.S. marshall right now." He took an extra badge from his pocket and handed it to Joe.

Joe closed his eyes, hoping that he was dreaming and that when he awoke he would be back in Marathon having coffee with Saber Entonelli.

But he knew that wouldn't happen when he heard Russak say: "Raise your right hand and repeat after me."

Chapter 7

Things hadn't gone anything as Joe Howard had wanted or hoped during the past two weeks. When he'd ridden out of Limpia Canyon that long ago, he was so positive that he could get the situation settled in no time at all. He would just ride into Marathon, find the cattle, arrest the one responsible for the bad meat going to the Indians, send Chief Keoni and his people good meat, and that would be the end of it.

Joe had found the cattle in Marathon with no problem. In fact, they had almost fallen into his lap. But there were so many people involved in the broken treaty with the Indians that it was hard for him to keep everyone straight in his mind. The only one he was sure about was Saber Entonelli.

Another amazing thing was that he'd just been made a deputy U.S. marshall. But that wasn't all. There was one more surprise in store for him.

Joe dropped his lanky frame down in a straight-backed chair across from McRaney's desk. Russak sat down in a similar chair by the opened window at the end of the office. The seating arrangement allowed each man a view of the other two without having to turn his head.

"When did Keoni and the others get here?" Joe asked, unbuckling the gunbelt and dropping it to the floor. He crossed his right ankle over his left knee.

"Late yesterday evening," McRaney answered, wincing in pain when he tried to stand up. That didn't work and he eased back down in the chair. "You won't believe what that Indian had me do."

Joe gave McRaney a patronizing glare and pulled his chin down toward his chest. "Eric," he said stoically, expelling a deep breath, "after what I've just learned right here in this office in the last ten minutes, I'd believe anything. But I know you're dying to tell me, so go ahead."

"Chief Keoni wanted me to put him in the guardhouse," the colonel said, stretching his arm out across the desk and rolling one thumb around the other.

"Why would he want you to do that?" Russak asked, leaning forward in the chair and bracing his elbows on his knees.

"He felt that if he was in the guardhouse," McRaney answered, shaking his head, "then he wouldn't be accused of doing anything wrong." McRaney looked at Joe across the desk. Each man already knew what the other was thinking.

"That Indian is the only person in this situation who hasn't done anything wrong," Joe said bitterly. Reaching down, he picked up his gun and rose stiffly

192

to his feet. "By all rights, Winston Haverty is the one who should be locked up. He had a Texas Ranger killed, plus is in with Powers in taking food away from the Indians." Anger swept over Joe and he gritted his teeth so hard he thought they would crack.

"We're going to take care of all that," McRaney said, bracing his hands palms down on the desk and standing up again. Reaching around, he picked up the crutches, which had thick leather pads at the top and a small wooden handle at hand level, positioned them under his arms, and hobbled slowly around the desk toward the door. "Winston Haverty insisted on one of the guest quarters. Before you begin arguing," McRaney said, stopping beside Joe, "I didn't want to antagonize that sawed-off snake before you got here. He told me about his part in all of this and that he'd signed a paper for you implicating Powers. Then he said, and this galls me to the core of my guts . . ." McRaney's voice dropped to a low growl and his mouth pulled into a snarl. "He wants some kind of immunity if he really testifies against Powers."

Joe's prediction had come true. The guilty always cries the loudest while the innocent suffer. He could feel anger boiling up in his stomach as he stood up and strapped the gunbelt back around his waist. A bitter taste rolled up into his mouth. He wished he didn't have to see Winston Haverty again. He'd be glad when this sorry business was finished.

"What kind of immunity?" Joe asked, holding his breath. He knew how much McRaney wanted Powers and was almost certain that he'd let Haverty go if he would testify against the senator.

"He wants his freedom for his testimony," McRaney answered, looking Joe straight in the eye. "But I told him that would be up to you. What are you going to do?" McRaney asked, pain beginning to dull his slate-blue eyes.

"I'm going to get Keoni out of that stupid guardhouse," Joe snapped, his eyes flashing. "He shouldn't have gone there in the first place. Then I think Russak and I should have a long talk with Rique Sanchez and Juan Gonzales. Where are they, by the way?" Joe did feel a little better that McRaney hadn't agreed to let Winston Haverty go.

Colonel McRaney leaned against the door and his face turned even whiter. "They didn't want to sleep in the barracks," he said, almost in a whisper. "I guess they didn't trust the soldiers any more than Keoni did. Joe, I've got to lie down. My leg is killing me. You know what to do. Just take care of it."

"What time do you want us to start for Alpine?" Joe asked, opening the door and feeling a little sorry for McRaney when he saw how much pain the colonel was in.

"Well, the sooner you leave, the sooner you'll get it done," McRaney replied pragmatically, expelling a shuddering breath. "I didn't know that one broken leg could hurt so bad."

The man looked as if he was going to pass out and Joe wondered how he'd gotten from his quarters to the office. Russak must have thought the same thing.

"Why don't you let us carry you to your place?" the marshall suggested, sympathy all over his thin face.

"How?" McRaney asked, frowning up hopefully at

the man who was even taller than he.

Russak stepped back into the office, got the armed chair, and put it behind McRaney. "It's as simple as sitting down," Russak answered, holding the back of the chair so that it wouldn't slip.

McRaney smiled when he saw what the marshall had in mind. Handing Joe his crutches, he eased down in the chair and leaned back. Sweat popped out on his face and it turned even whiter.

Russak was about six inches taller than Joe and bent over to match his height so that the chair wouldn't be lopsided. They got a lot of stares, whistles, and hollers as they carried McRaney aross the dusty parade ground. But they reached his small white framed house in half the time it would have taken the colonel to hobble that far. The colonel probably couldn't have made it anyway.

"There's some laudanum in the cabinet in the kitchen," McRaney said, easing up from the chair and down on the bed with a light blue spread.

"If I were you," Joe said, coming back with the brown bottle and a spoon, "I'd stay on that bed for at least two days. You're doing yourself more harm than good with all of that banging around you're doing. That leg needs to be propped up and given a lot of rest." Joe got a blanket from a chair, doubled it up, gently picked up McRaney's leg, and put the blanket under it.

"You're probably right," McRaney agreed, taking a spoonful of the medicine and making a bad face. "Anything that tastes that bad has to work."

"You really don't have anything to worry about,"

Russak said, hooking his thumbs over his belt. There was humor in his green eyes under the reddish-brown brows. "You have an Indian chief, two Mexicans, a deputy U.S. marshall, and a U.S. marshall to take care of things for you. Just lie back and take it easy." A grin pulled at his thin mouth.

"You lucky devil," Joe said, laughing down at McRaney. The colonel took off his coat and lay back against the pillow, a resigned expression on his long face. A little color was beginning to creep back into it. McRaney's eyes began closing and Joe and Russak walked toward the door.

Joe felt sorry for the colonel as he looked over his shoulder at the sleeping man. He had always thought that Eric McRaney would be able to ride a tornado then use it for a whip. Now one throw from a horse had finally put him down for a while.

"I'm going to get Chief Keoni out of the guardhouse," Joe said to Russak, who had picked up the chair and followed him out of McRaney's house. "There's no point in him staying in there."

Joe kicked through the dust back across the parade ground toward the guardhouse. Russak had gone back to McRaney's office with the chair. Joe was almost to the rock and wooden structure when he heard his name called. He turned around to see Winston Haverty hurrying toward him as fast as his short legs would carry him. His tan hat was at an arrogant angle on his yellow head and Joe wished that he was half as important as Haverty thought he was.

"What are you going to do?" Haverty asked,

mopping his damp face with a tan handkerchief.

"I'm going to get Keoni out of there," Joe answered, nodding toward the small cell. He wanted to hit the little man standing before him so hard that he could actually taste it. "He doesn't need to be in there." Haverty reached out and caught hold of Joe's arm to stop him.

"Get your hands off me before I rip your arm off and give you the beating you deserve," Joe snapped, jerking his arm free of Haverty's grip. His eyes were blazing. Before he knew what he was doing, Joe reached out, grabbed a handful of Winston Haverty's white shirt, and yanked the wide-eyed man toward him. "When did you have the time to tell Sheriff Jagger in Brewster to send a telegram to Marshall Russak? Why did you tell him I was responsible for the death of Jack Lucas?"

Joe didn't know if it was Haverty's sudden peril or the mention of the telegram that drained the color from his face. He began breathing hard.

"I don't know what you're talking about," Haverty said just before Joe popped him squarely in the face with his left hand.

Joe felt good when he saw blood begin trickling from Haverty's thin nose. "You know exactly what I'm talking about," Joe countered in a cold, low voice. "You knew that I'd eventually go back to Marathon for the paper in your desk. You had that poor excuse of a sheriff in Brewster send a telegram to marshall Russak to arrest me for killing Jack Lucas. I overheard you and Graff talking at the cattle pens in Brewster and I know that you had Cavazos kill Lucas.

You're no better than a snake. You belong in there instead of Keoni. But I'm not going to put you in there yet. You're going to help me get Senator Caleb Powers."

A snide smile slid across Haverty's small face as he wiped the blood away. He looked up at Joe with temerity in his small eyes.

"I don't have to help you do anything," Haverty said, confident sarcasm in his voice. "I signed a piece of paper under duress. I was brought to this godforsaken place called a fort as the hostage of an Indian and two Mexicans. Whatever you might have heard can't be used against me because it is hearsay. You are only an army scout and I don't have to do anything you tell me."

At that very minute, Joe Howard wished he owned the miserable little cattle thief and could have sold him for what he thought he was worth. Joe wouldn't have to work again for the rest of his life.

But Joe knew that whatever was up, whether it was confidence, ego, or a leaf, always had to come down. Joe had felt good when he'd smacked Haverty in the face. But what he was about to do to him now would make him feel great!

"I have been deputized as a U.S. marshall," Joe said, cocking his head to one side and narrowing his eyes. He took the tin star from his pocket. "I can arrest you right now for complicity in a Texas Ranger's death. But I don't want to do that. I want to get Caleb Powers for Colonel McRaney, and by God, you're going to help me do it!"

Winston Haverty froze where he stood. His eyes

would never be that wide again. He knew that Joe wasn't joking and he also knew from the hot look in the army scout's eyes that if he didn't help him, he would probably shoot him.

Joe moved over to the cell and asked the guard for the key.

"It hasn't been locked," the young private said, a tender smile on his blistered face. "The chief just thinks it is. He could have gotten out any time he wanted."

Joe opened the door and looked inside in total disbelief. Instead of sitting on the wooden bunk or the low stool, Chief Keoni was sitting on the floor in a dim corner, leaning back against the wall.

"Why are you sitting on the floor, Chief," Joe asked, stepping into the cell.

"No one can see me if I sit down here," Keoni replied, blinking his dark eyes as the light flooded in on him. "If no one knows where I am, I not be blamed for anything."

Joe expelled a disgruntled breath and shook his head in exasperation. "Come on out, Chief," Joe said, bending down and taking hold of his arm to help him up. "No one is going to accuse you of anything. Everything is just about over and soon you won't have to worry about your people having enough meat to eat. A U.S. marshall is going to help us."

Keoni held Joe's gaze as he stood up and Joe knew that Keoni didn't believe any more of what he said than Joe did when he said it. There would always be something for the Indians to worry about.

"Marshall Russak, Winston Haverty, and I are

going to Alpine tomorrow to arrest Senator Powers," Joe said, leading the way toward the mess hall. He was sure that Keoni hadn't eaten all day and he must be hungry. Joe was famished. The coffee and meat they'd had that morning had worn off. "Do you want to go with us? It will be on your way back to Elephant Mountain."

Joe thought that Keoni would enjoy hearing the senator try to defend himself.

"You not say anything about McRaney," Keoni reminded him, pulling back as they neared the long building where the aroma of beans, meat, and fresh bread poured through the windows.

"I not go in there," Keoni said, shaking his head adamantly before Joe could answer his question about McRaney. There was anxiety in his dark eyes.

"Oh, now Chief," Joe cajoled, having some idea what was going on in his mind. "I ate with you a few days ago. The least you can do is eat with me now. You might like it."

Winston Haverty had followed closely behind but went on inside while the two men talked. Keoni stepped inside but moved over by the door and stopped. Even though he stood tall and proud, he seemed nervous and uncertain about what to do.

Joe, probably having some idea what was going through the chief's mind, because he would no doubt have felt the same way if he'd been in the Indian's moccasins, went over to the long table and picked up two plates. On one he put two pieces of fried meat, mashed potatoes, greens, a knife, and a fork. On the other plate he put just three pieces of meat and a fork, just in case Keoni wanted to use it.

There were two straight-backed chairs by the stove and he dragged them over by a window. Here, they would be away from the soldiers and Haverty. Joe knew that Keoni was probably bothered more by the soldiers than he was by the little man chowing down on a big piece of meat.

Joe sat down on one chair and wondered if Keoni would sit on the other or use the floor. Joe smiled up at the Indian when he took the plate from his extended hand and actually sat down on the chair.

Joe watched Keoni from the corner of his eye to see how he'd eat the steak. He wasn't very surprised when the Indian picked up a piece of meat with his fingers and smelled it before taking a small bite. Keoni chewed slowly then swallowed. Looking up, he met the expectant look in Joe's eyes and nodded.

"Taste good," Keoni said, taking another bite and chewing more zestfully. "Indian woman not cook like this. How you fix?" This time he took a bigger bite.

"It's easy," Joe answered, shrugging his shoulders and putting a forkful of potatoes, then greens into his mouth and swallowing before continuing. "Just put some lard in a hot pan over a fire and cook it until it's done."

"I will tell women," Keoni said, nodding. "We only boil or eat meat raw."

Joe stopped, the fork halfway to his mouth at Keoni's last statement. His stomach turned over at the thought of putting raw meat into his mouth and chewing it. He still hadn't forgotten the stench of the

201

rotten meat from the other day and this didn't help matters much.

"You ever eat horse?" Keoni asked as nonchalantly as a man of his bearing could. He was now devouring the second piece of meat.

"Nope," Joe answered, laying the fork on the plate. His appetite was completely gone now. The meal would have been a total waste if it hadn't been for the cup of strong black coffee.

"So," Joe said, swallowing a large sip of coffee, "do you want to ride to Alpine when we go after Senator Powers? It will be on the way back to your village." Keoni hadn't given him an answer yet. Keoni put the meat down on the plate and wiped his fingers on his pants. He seemed to give the invitation a lot of thought before he finally nodded his answer.

"I would like very much," he said, turning his head away but moving his black eyes back to Joe. "Want to see white man who hate Indian so much to send bad meat all time."

A look that Joe couldn't describe crossed the Indian's bronze face. It wasn't anger. It wasn't hatred. It wasn't sadness. Maybe a combination of all three.

"You don't have to sleep in the guardhouse, you know," Joe said, standing up and looking down at Keoni. "If no one has taken it, there is an empty bunk next to mine in the barracks."

Once again Keoni gave Joe's words a lot of thought before he spoke. "I will sleep in long room," he finally said, handing Joe his plate and standing up, the other piece of steak in his hand. "But not sleep on wood bed." He shook his head and rubbed his back.

"Ground and blankets better for back."

As Joe had guessed, a few surprised brows arched when he and Keoni walked into the barracks.

"Why are you bringing him in here?" a surly-looking sergeant asked, curling up his mustached lip. "He's probably got fleas."

"If he does," Joe shot back, giving the man a castigating look, "he must have gotten too close to you." Loud laughter bounced off the walls and the sergeant ducked his head, embarrassed at being the butt of his own joke.

Joe's bunk was along the wall by the open window. The other bunk was on the opposite side. Joe took off his hat, shirt, boots, and socks and stretched out on the wool blanket over the thin mattress. Trying not to be too obvious, Joe turned his head, and in the dimness of the two oil lamps by the door, he watched Chief Keoni take the blankets from the mattress, push them under the bunk, then slide in on top of them. Doing this, he was sure he would be out of everyone's way and no one would bother him.

Joe had one more thing to wonder about before he went to sleep and that was where Sanchez and Gonzales were. He hadn't seen them since getting to the fort. Joe didn't know or care where Winston Haverty spent the night.

But the little man was one of the first people he saw when he and Keoni went to the mess hall the next morning. He was pretty sure that Marshall Russak had slept at Colonel McRaney's quarters because he saw him coming out the door as Joe went in to eat.

"How is the colonel this morning?" Joe asked

Russak as the tall marshall filled his plate much like Joe's with fried eggs, ham, gravy, and biscuits. Keoni was sitting to Joe's right with only ham and a biscuit on his plate.

"I don't know," Russak answered, swallowing a mouthful of eggs and bread. "I opened his door a while ago and he was still sleeping. He must have taken some more of that medicine after I left last night. I went by to ask him a little more about Powers and he invited me to sleep on the sofa. It lacked a foot from being long enough so I slept on the floor. How soon do you want to leave?"

Joe put the last of the ham and egg into his mouth and washed it down with coffee. "As soon as we can get saddled up," Joe answered, glancing at Keoni. He must not have liked the ham as much as the steak. There was still an extra piece on the plate that he pushed back. He stood up when the other two men did.

"Let's go, Haverty," Joe said, looking down at him and settling the Colt .45 around his waist. He saw Haverty hesitate and moved his hand down to the pistol handle. Haverty, knowing he couldn't refuse, stood up and followed the three men out to the corral. Joe was amazed to see Rique Sanchez and Juan Gonzales waiting there for them.

"Marshall, do you think there's any need for Sanchez and Gonzales to come with us?" Joe asked Russak. The two men had only been hired to drive some cattle somewhere. They had done their part and it wouldn't be necessary for them to go along unless they actually wanted to. Joe had all he needed in his pockets with the papers implicating Powers and he had Winston Haverty along, as well.

"Do you men want to go to Alpine with us?" Russak asked, a congenial smile on his long, thin face.

The two Mexicans exchanged looks and Joe was glad when they suddenly shook their heads at the same time. That would be two less for him to worry about. Something told him that someone would get killed today. He just prayed to God that it wouldn't be him.

Six men rode out the stone gates of Fort Davis, and Joe Howard sensed that only one, or maybe two, of them would ever see the place again. Two of the men, Sanchez and Gonzales, would be the only two who would be unscathed by the outcome of what would happen in Alpine tomorrow. As soon as they were out of the canyon, Sanchez and Gonzales turned their horses toward Marathon.

The sun was a little past noon when they crossed a small stream and decided that it would be a good time to stop, rest the horses, and have something to eat.

"Something has been bothering me, Haverty," Joe said, taking the coffeepot from the grub sack and pouring water into it.

"What?" Haverty asked, a sullen scowl on his face. "What could possibly be bothering you about me? I thought you would have everything all figured out."

If Winston Haverty hadn't been so short, Joe would have liked nothing better than to give him a sound beating for his obstinence. But the very least he could do to him was give him a good spanking.

"Why haven't you tried to escape the past couple of days?" Joe asked, glaring at the yellow-haired man through narrowed eyes. "You weren't under any guard and you weren't tied to anything."

Haverty shot Joe a reproachful look and shook his head slowly before answering. "Look around you," he said wearily, waving his arm in a semicircle to indicate the skyscraping mountains and the vast desert beyond. "How far do you really think I would get? Either the soldiers would find me or that Indian"—Haverty paused, pulling his mouth into a sickening snarl—"would have his men track me down. Regardless of what's going to happen to me, I'm better off with you two."

From the first time that Joe had met Winston Haverty, he had guessed him to be a smart man. Joe was even more sure of that fact now. Joe knew, on the other hand, that if it had been him in Haverty's boots, he would have taken his chances and been long gone by now. A man could live a lifetime in these mountains without ever having to see another human being if he didn't want to. There were other things besides a gun and knife that could be used for protection.

Marshall Russak had been quiet all this time. He'd fried some meat and made flat bread while Joe and Haverty had been arguing. Pouring coffee into a cup, he sat down on the ground and leaned against the trunk of a cottonwood tree.

"I really can't see where a law has been broken," Russak said, putting a piece of meat between two slices of bread and taking a bite. "Some cattle were gotten together. Then different people got some of the cattle. What's the big deal?"

Joe looked down at the marshall as if he had two heads. Apparently no one had gone into exact details about the situation.

"If you believe that no law has been broken," Joe raged, pouring coffee into a cup and glaring at Russak, "then you've got another thing coming. Let me explain it to you." Sarcastic disbelief narrowed Joe's eyes.

Even though it was wasting time and it irritated Joe Howard to have to do it, he explained how cattle were bought from Silas Bruell through Powers and Haverty to be given to the Indians at specific intervals during the year. Apparently Senator Powers had been the government official doing the buying. He had either seen an opportunity to take part of the cattle and begin a herd of his own or sell them to buyers elsewhere. The cattle he got had been the pick of the herd.

Winston Haverty must have been the middleman. For his part in it, he got the second-best cattle. Joe knew for a fact that those cattle were to be shipped from Brewster to someone in Chicago for a hefty profit.

That left the poor, starving Indians to get the worst of the meat.

"Haverty, tell Russak what kind of meat you tasted the other day in Keoni's village," Joe said snidely, pausing for a long breath after he'd finished his narration. His stomach turned over as he remembered the look, smell, and feel of the meat that Powers and Haverty had wanted the Indians to eat.

Once again, if looks could killed, Joe Howard would have become a corpse. The little man's face turned white and he swallowed hard as he remembered the rancid meat that Joe had forced him to put into his mouth.

"It's true," Haverty conceded, looking down at the ground. "Powers said that if the Indians were kept hungry, they wouldn't have enough strength to raid wagon trains and stagecoaches and houses."

Anger, like hot water, washed over Joe. The Indians had agreed to stop doing all those things if the government would help them with food. Most of the buffalo were gone. The big, shaggy animals had been one of the mainstays of the Indians' way of life. But as progress and greed had pushed the Indians back, their source of food, lodging, and clothing had been virtually depleted.

To Joe's way of thinking, the Indian had no choice. He had to fight or starve. Live or die. Any sane man would do the same if his family was threatened.

A different expression crossed Russak's long, thin face. He looked down at the coffee cup in his hands. Deep lines formed between his brows. Raising his head, he switched his bewildered gaze from Joe, over to Haverty, and back to Joe again.

"I wasn't aware that all that had been going on," Russak said, shaking his head wearily. "I just thought that Howard and McRaney had some kind of grudge against Powers and that's why he was going after him. I've known Caleb Powers for a long time and he just doesn't seem to be that kind of person."

Joe wanted to hit Russak as much as he'd wanted to tear into Winston Haverty earlier.

"Didn't you think it was a little strange," Joe said in a sarcastic voice, "when the sheriff in Brewster sent you a telegram and described me almost down to my toenails as the one who'd killed a Texas Ranger? I was the one who had told him how the Ranger had died in the first place and that Armando Cavazos had done it. When this entire situation is settled, I suggest you have a long talk with Sheriff Pierce Jagger."

Joe was so angry that knots stood out on both sides of his whiskered face and his mouth was pressed into a tight line. He knew that if he didn't calm down, it would only be him and Keoni who were left to ride into Alpine after Senator Caleb Powers. But then he would be in real trouble for killing a marshall. He had thought that a marshall would have been more on top of what was going on in his town.

Chief Keoni had been silent and somber all this time, chewing on the piece of steak from last night. Joe wondered how the Indians would handle a matter like this. Something told him that it wouldn't be this way.

"Howard," Russak said, grunting as he stood up, "a U.S. marshall can't be everywhere at once. Every once in a while, something does get by us." He must have read Joe's thoughts.

They had wasted too much time arguing and it was getting on Joe's nerves. He wanted to hurry and get things done. Draining the coffeepot, he stood up and helped Russak clean and pack the utensils in the grub sack. Haverty hadn't made a move to do anything.

Since Chief Keoni's horse didn't have a saddle to be replaced and he had carried the extra piece of steak inside his shirt, there was nothing for him to do except mount up.

The four men could have reached Alpine late that night if they'd kept riding but decided to stop early when they reached a river with lush green grass for the horses and a lot of shade from cottonwood trees for them.

Each man probably knew that they'd argued enough earlier and also knew that more wouldn't solve anything. After the horses had been watered and hobbled in the grass, each man sat down on the ground and either went to sleep or became lost in his own thoughts.

Keoni, taking the last piece of steak from his shirt, got up and walked down to the river. He waded out a short distance and looked like a clothed statue as he squatted down. Suddenly his right hand slashed through the water. When he stood up, he was holding a catfish. He tossed it up on the bank with a hard throw and repeated the procedure three more times. What he would call a grin was on his face as he came back to the men, who had watched, almost in awe.

"Supper," he said, his black eyes twinkling. "I get wet. I catch. You clean. You cook." He looked down at Joe.

For the moment Joe believed that Keoni was at peace with the entire world. He was joking and smiling. Joe wished that it could always be that way for this man with the austere bearing standing before him. But he knew that couldn't be. Some other white men would come along and tear down what was being built up.

Haverty and Russak's laughter joined in with his and Keoni's, and Joe knew that by this time tomorrow this jovial mood would be only a memory.

"You've got a deal, Chief," Joe said, rubbing his hands together and getting to his feet. "I haven't had fish in a long time. Too bad we don't have cornbread."

Gathering up the four fish, Joe took them down to the river and cleaned them. When he got back to the others, Russak had made a fire, took the fish from Joe, and put them in a pan. It didn't take long for the fish to disappear. Haverty even ate his.

Night was settling over the mountains and creeping up the granite pinnacles, and long shadows were crawling across the ground. Their blankets felt good against the chilly wind and Joe wished that he were back at the barracks on his bunk. It seemed hard only when he was sleeping on it.

He'd been sure that, with so many things on his mind, he wouldn't be able to sleep at all that night. But instead, and his full stomach probably had a great deal to do with it, he went to sleep almost as soon as his head touched the saddle. His dreams were even pleasant.

He and Saber were sitting by a stream much like

the one where they were now. The cottonwood trees were filled with singing birds and everything was right with the world. Joe didn't awaken until he was being shaken by the shoulder the next morning.

Keoni was standing over him. The sun was just peeping over the mountains, touching the jagged peaks with pink, orange, and yellow. A few cotton-ball clouds eased along on the early morning breeze.

An impending dread pulled a knot in Joe's stomach as he sat up and rolled his blankets together. Everything seemed extra quiet around them. Joe glanced around at Keoni. The Indian seemed nervous. Joe didn't know if that was the correct description for the Indian. He stood straight as he always did. But this time, he seemed more rigid.

In the growing light, Joe could see around him better. Russak was turning over to get up. But Winston Haverty was lying facedown on the ground a few feet from where Joe had been sleeping.

He hadn't been there last night. Then Joe felt sick to his stomach. A knife handle was sticking out of the center of his white shirt in his back. Dried blood marred the shirt even more in a wide circle. In Haverty's clenched right hand was a short-handled, long-bladed knife.

Joe wondered where he had gotten it. He knew that Haverty's pistol and knives had been taken away from him when he and Bernie Graff had been searched the other day. Bending down for a closer look, Joe saw that it was like those in the mess hall back at Fort Davis.

No wonder I slept so well last night, Joe gave

himself time to think before cold shivers ran over his entire body. Keoni was watching over me.

"What in the devil happened?" Joe asked, looking quickly from the still body on the ground to the stolid Indian standing before him, a calmer expression on his face now.

"I awake," Keoni said, looking over at Russak, who was awake now and getting to his feet. The marshall put on his hat and did a double-take when he saw the body on the ground.

"I saw him," Keoni continued, nodding toward Haverty. "He had knife in hand and was going to put in your back." Keoni looked back at Joe. "He not hear me. When he raise hand with knife, I kill him."

"What's going on here?" Russak asked, disbelief gaping his mouth and bulging his eyes.

Joe took and expelled a long breath. He'd had attempts made against his life before, but never while he slept.

"Haverty tried to kill me," Joe said simply, pulling air in through his clenched teeth. He was more shaken than he wanted to admit. His hands were almost shaking.

"Why do you suppose he wanted to do something like that?" Russak asked, squatting down by Haverty's body. It took a strong tug to pull the knife out of Haverty's back. He must have been able to tell from the markings on the handle that it belonged to Keoni. Without saying anything, he rubbed the knife in the sand, then handed it up to the Indian.

"Maybe he really thought that it would still be his word against mine when we get to Alpine," Joe answered in a low voice. Turning, he went to Haverty's blankets, picked up both of them, and went back to where Russak had turned Haverty over. Keoni, still holding his knife by the handle and pointing it toward the ground, was standing a few feet away. His bronze face was immobile.

"You're probably right," Russak conceded, taking one blanket and spreading it out on the ground. He and Joe rolled Haverty's body onto it, then wrapped the other blanket around it. With no other choice, they piled rocks around the body. When they'd finished, they decided to saddle up and ride on some distance before stopping to cook anything for breakfast.

Like Fort Davis, Alpine was surrounded by mountains. The town, like most in the West, was small. It consisted of the usual barbershop, saloon, dry goods store, bank, hotel, and transportation facilities.

The likeliest place for the senator to be, if he didn't have a private residence, would be the hotel or maybe a roominghouse.

The gray, three-story Cinnabar Hotel was at the end of the street, next to the Drayfuss Restaurant. The hotel was where Joe pulled Serge to a stop first. Even though Russak was in charge as far as the law went, Joe felt that since he'd started out on this job two weeks ago by himself, it was still his. He didn't see Russak arch his brows when he swung down, tied Serge, and went into the hotel. Not that it would have really mattered to him.

"Does Senator Caleb Powers live here?" Joe asked

the desk clerk, who'd come from the back with a fixed smile and expectant gleam in his eyes. "If he doesn't, can you tell me where."

"Senator Powers has a small but nice ranch south of town," the man answered, obvious pride in his voice that he knew something personal about the senator. A bitter taste rolled up into Joe's mouth as he turned to leave the hotel lobby. He knew that it would be a sure bet where the cattle for his "small but nice ranch" had come from. Maybe the Indians could come and live on the ranch after Powers was ousted. This impossible thought brought a grin across Joe's face. He still hadn't realized that he'd overstepped his authority.

"Powers lives south of here," Joe said to the questioning look in Russak's green eyes. Joe was glad now that he still carried the paper from Haverty's office with Powers's name on it. Without it, they couldn't do much of anything. Even though he had Haverty's signed statement in his pocket also, the senator could say that Joe had forced Haverty to sign it. Joe would only have his word to the contrary.

"How do you want to work this?" Russak asked, breaking into Joe's thoughts.

"I think we should confront him with our suspicions and then arrest him," Joe answered. That sounded so simple, said a little voice in the back of Joe's mind. But deep down in his soul, he knew it wouldn't be. He'd been around Colonel Eric McRaney too long and was beginning to think like him.

"We should make him eat bad meat," Chief Keoni said, riding his horse up beside Joe. He had been riding behind the two men all this time. The only time they were aware of his presence was when he actually said something to them.

"That's not a bad idea," Joe said, turning his head and laughing at the Indian.

Either the income from being a senator or being in the cattle business had really paid off for Senator Caleb Powers. Somehow Joe got the impression that it was the latter. Honest politicians couldn't make the kind of money to afford what Joe was looking at.

The desk clerk had said "small ranch." If what Joe was looking at belonged to the senator, there were at least a hundred acres spread out in the surprisingly green valley below them. Fat, healthy, shiny-skinned cattle, some that Joe recognized from the pens in Marathon, ambled slowly along, feeding on grass made green by a flowing river. A low white adobe house with arches across the front and a red cobblestoned roof bespoke of a good life. Flowers and cactus with yellow blooms on them were planted around the house.

Joe and Russak rode up to the house, dismounted, and tied their horses. Joe knocked on the dark paneled door. Keoni had pulled his horse to a stop about twenty yards from the house under a cottonwood tree. A middle-aged Mexican man, dressed all in white and wearing leather sandals, opened the door, a subservient smile on his brown face.

"Is Senator Powers here?" Joe asked, his heart slamming against his ribs. He knew that this wasn't going to be easy and was actually glad that Russak was along. Joe knew that this was the point that he had been riding toward ever since he'd left Fort Davis two weeks ago. It was time for a showdown with Powers, and Joe wished that Colonel Eric McRaney could have been there as well.

"Senator Powers is out at the corral, señor," the Mexican answered in a low voice. Joe noticed that he stiffened when he saw the metal stars on his and Russak's shirts. "It is at the back of the casa," he continued, batting his eyes quickly.

"Why don't you go around the west side of the house," Joe suggested to Russak, "and I'll go around this way." Joe looked around at Keoni. The Indian was still sitting on his horse.

"Good idea," Russak acknowledged, pulling his hat down low over his thin forehead.

Joe settled the leather gunbelt more comfortably around his waist and loosened the Colt .45 in the holster. He didn't see anybody at the corral as he walked around the east side of the house. If Powers was around, he had to be in the well-constructed barn to the right of the corral, where four golden Palominos with white manes and tails were chomping on a bale of hay. They, too, were enjoying the good life.

Joe, wondering where the ranch hands were, had reached the front of the barn just as Russak came around the west side of the house.

"Since you know this low-down snake," Joe said to Russak in a strained voice, "you call him." Joe still couldn't believe that they were here to arrest a government official. But he didn't know why he was so surprised. There had been crooked politicians

217

since the beginning of time and it would probably continue until the end of time.

"Caleb, this is Carl Russak," the marshall called out. His given name sounded strange in Joe's ears. Up until now he'd only been "Russak" to Joe. "Caleb. Are you in there? Come on out." Russak had his hand on the handle of the .38 at his side.

The barn door swung open on well-oiled hinges and a man, who was not quite what Joe had imagined Senator Caleb Powers to look like, came out.

Colonel McRaney had always described Powers as pompous and arrogant. To Joe, that meant someone tall with silver hair, black brows and beady blue eyes. This Senator Powers wasn't quite as tall as Russak. But he was muscular and looked hard. The sleeves of his dark brown shirt were tight around his thick arms. The silver hair was there, but the eyes were brown under hooded dark brown brows. Black gabardine pants fitted his muscular legs, and hand-tooled boots and a black leather vest did give him a pompous appearance indeed. Something told Joe that Powers knew how to use the pearl-handled Smith & Wesson .38 strapped around his lean waist.

"Carl, what in the devil are you doing out here?" Powers asked, drawing his brows together in a straight line over a thin nose. He walked toward Russak, his right hand extended for a shake. "It's been a long time." A smile began on his tanned face but faded and he dropped his hand when he looked over at Joe and saw the star on his shirt. He raised his eyes to the badge on Russak's shirt. Powers looked up at Russak and eased his hand down to the pistol at his side. "This isn't a social call, is it?" he asked, narrowing his eyes.

"No, it isn't, Caleb," Russak answered, shaking his head slowly. "I'm sorry."

Joe wished that Russak would stop all this pussyfooting around and get on with it. Powers didn't need any apologies. He should be the one apologizing to the Indians. He needed to be shot where he stood! If Russak didn't hurry up and arrest the haughty man frowning there, that was exactly what Joe was going to do.

"What are you getting at?" Powers asked, the frown darkening on his wide tanned face. He switched his gaze over to Joe, then back to Russak.

"You are under arrest for violating a government treaty with the Apache Chief Keoni," Russak said. He paused for a deep breath.

Powers surprised both Joe and Russak when he threw back his head and roared in laughter until his eyes smarted. He sobered when he saw their solemn expressions.

"You're joking," Powers finally said, regaining his composure. He blinked his eyes and coughed. "How in the world did you get such a ridiculous idea?" He let his thin mouth slide into a grin. Pompous was a good description for him now.

"From this," Joe said caustically, wanting to jerk the colt .45 from the holster and blow the smiling man out of his boots. He removed the paper from his pocket and held it out for Powers to see. Joe wished that Eric McRaney could have seen the look on

Powers's face. Joe watched the color drain from the senator's face as the reality of the implicating paper hit him.

"Drop the gunbelt, Caleb," Russak said, his green eyes boring into Powers. "You are under arrest."

"Don't be a fool, Carl," Powers said, a cunning in his eyes and voice. "Put up that gun and we'll talk. I'll make you a partner in all this if you forget about what you saw on that paper." He made a broad sweep with his arm that included the ranch, the cattle, and the house.

"What do you mean, partner?" Russak asked, his eyes narrowing as he lowered his head a fraction.

"The government *is* buying a lot of cattle for the Indians," Powers said sarcastically. "I've been paying Winston Haverty to send half the cattle to me and the other half to the Indians."

Joe and Russak exchanged startled looks. Apparently Powers didn't know that Haverty had been double-crossing him and sending him only a third of the cattle.

"Haverty has been sending you only a third of the cattle," Joe said cynically, watching a red color easing up Powers's face. "They *have* been the best cattle. The Indians have been getting the worst of the bunch. Haverty has been selling the other third and putting the money in his own pocket."

For Joe, standing out there in the hot sun, with the sweat running down his back, was worth the disbelief, then fury that darkened Powers's face. The senator's eyes darkened and he pulled his mouth into a tight, white-rimmed circle.

"I'll kill Haverty when I get my hands on him," Powers threatened through clenched teeth.

"Chief Keoni has already beat you to it," Russak said, leveling the Remington at Powers again. "Like I said, you're under arrest."

"The devil I am," Powers roared, a cold look now in his brown eyes. He took a step backward, and at the same time, with a speed that would match or might even beat Joe's, he jerked the Smith & Wesson from the holster, aimed from the hip, and fired. The bullet caught U.S. Marshall Carl Russak squarely in the chest.

Clutching at the front of his shirt, Russak seemed to hang suspended in midair, then fell facedown in the dirt. Maybe things would have been different if Russak had disarmed Powers from the very beginning. But they'd never know about that now. Marshall Carl Russak was dead.

The sound of the exploding gun brought the whiteclad Mexican hurrying out the back door. Joe heard hoofbeats coming around the east side of the house and knew that Keoni was riding up. But Joe didn't take the time to look around to be sure. Jerking the Colt .45 from the holster, Joe aimed it at Powers and pulled the trigger.

Powers took a step back and the bullet that would have struck him in the chest caught him in the stomach. Powers aimed his pistol at Joe but fell backward on the ground as the gun fired. Joe heard the bullet whistle past his head. Powers grabbed for his stomach as the gun fell from his hand.

Joe holstered the .45 and dropped to his knee on

221

the ground by Powers. He looked like any other dying man lying in the dirt. He was trying to say something.

"Why?" Joe asked, bending closer to hear him. "Why did you kill Russak?"

"I wasn't going to let him arrest me over a bunch of stinking Indians," Powers gasped, digging his fingers in the ground. "If the Indians left to find meat somewhere else, more whites could come out here." Powers coughed and a clot of blood erupted from his mouth.

"Why don't you like Indians?" Joe asked, having no pity for this obviously prejudiced and dying man.

"Because they're such savages and . . ." Powers's voice trailed off. His body stiffened for a second, then relaxed. Senator Caleb Powers was dead.

Chief Keoni dismounted and walked slowly toward Joe.

"He dead?" Keoni stated more than asked. Joe nodded and stood up. He still couldn't understand where all the ranch hands were. But that didn't matter now.

The houseman hurried over to Powers and stared down at him.

"Get a blanket and cover him up," Joe said, no remorse in his voice. "Get someone to help you bury him. Chief, go get the marshall's horse. We'll bury him somewhere else."

Keoni turned the horse around, and in only a few minutes, he was back with both horses. He helped Joe lay the marshall's body across the saddle and tie a blanket around it.

"What about cattle?" Keoni asked, nodding his head toward the river.

"All of those belong to you," Joe said, expelling a long breath. "Do you want me to help you drive them to your village or do you want me to wait until you go and get your men and come back?"

A small, amused grin twinkled in Chief Keoni's black eyes. "You ride the moon south for me once, Joe Howard. My braves will help you now. They have followed you all the time."

Chief Keoni raised his right arm and seemingly from out of nowhere appeared at least twenty braves.

Reaching over, Joe slapped Keoni on the shoulder. Joe's job and the Indians' hunger were over. Joe would head toward Marathon and go fishing.

POWELL'S ARMY
BY TERENCE DUNCAN

#1: UNCHAINED LIGHTNING   (1994, $2.50)
Thundering out of the past, a trio of deadly enforcers dispenses its own brand of frontier justice throughout the untamed American West! Two men and one woman, they are the U.S. Army's most lethal secret weapon—they are POWELL'S ARMY!

#2: APACHE RAIDERS   (2073, $2.50)
The disappearance of seventeen Apache maidens brings tribal unrest to the violent breaking point. To prevent an explosion of bloodshed, Powell's Army races through a nightmare world south of the border—and into the deadly clutches of a vicious band of Mexican flesh merchants!

#3: MUSTANG WARRIORS   (2171, $2.50)
Someone is selling cavalry guns and horses to the Comanche—and that spells trouble for the bluecoats' campaign against Chief Quanah Parker's bloodthirsty Kwahadi warriors. But Powell's Army are no strangers to trouble. When the showdown comes, they'll be ready—and someone is going to die!

#4: ROBBERS ROOST   (2285, $2.50)
After hijacking an army payroll wagon and killing the troopers riding guard, Three-Fingered Jack and his gang high-tail it into Virginia City to spend their ill-gotten gains. But Powell's Army plans to apprehend the murderous hardcases before the local vigilantes do—to make sure that Jack and his slimy band stretch hemp the legal way!

Available wherever paperbacks are sold, or order direct from the Publisher. Send cover price plus 50¢ per copy for mailing and handling to Zebra Books, Dept. 3421, 475 Park Avenue South, New York, N.Y. 10016. Residents of New York, New Jersey and Pennsylvania must include sales tax. DO NOT SEND CASH.